NEW YORK REVIEW BOOKS
CLASSICS

FAMILY *and* BORGHESIA

NATALIA GINZBURG (1916–1991) was born Natalia Levi in Palermo, Sicily, the daughter of a Jewish biologist father and a Catholic mother. She grew up in Turin, in a household that was a salon for antifascist activists, intellectuals, and artists, and published her first short stories at the age of eighteen; she would go on to become one of the most important and widely taught writers in Italy, taking up the themes of oppression, family, and social change. In 1938, she married Leone Ginzburg, a prominent Turinese writer, activist, and editor. In 1940, the fascist government exiled the Ginzburgs and their three children to a remote village in Abruzzo. After the fall of Mussolini, Leone fled to Rome, where he was arrested by Nazi authorities and tortured to death. Natalia married Gabriele Baldini, an English professor, in 1950, and spent the next three decades in Rome, London, and Turin, writing dozens of novels, plays, and essays. *Lessico famigliare* (*Family Lexicon*) won the prestigious Strega Prize in 1963 and *La famiglia Manzoni* was awarded the 1984 Bagutta Prize. From 1983 to 1987, she served in the Italian parliament as an Independent (having left the Communist Party), where she dedicated herself to reformist causes, including food prices and Palestinian rights.

BERYL STOCKMAN is a translator, poet, and professional psychic and tarot reader. She lives in London.

ERIC GUDAS is the author of *Best Western and Other Poems*. His essays and reviews have appeared in *Raritan*, *All About Jazz*, *Poetry Flash*, *Senses of Cinema*, *The Bloomsbury Review*, and the *Los Angeles Review of Books*, where he is a contributing editor.

FAMILY
and BORGHESIA

Two Novellas

NATALIA GINZBURG

Translated from the Italian by
BERYL STOCKMAN

Afterword by
ERIC GUDAS

NEW YORK REVIEW BOOKS

New York

THIS IS A NEW YORK REVIEW BOOK
PUBLISHED BY THE NEW YORK REVIEW OF BOOKS
435 Hudson Street, New York, NY 10014
www.nyrb.com

Family was originally published in the Italian language as *Famiglia*.
First published as an NYRB Classic in 2021.

Library of Congress Cataloging-in-Publication Data
Names: Ginzburg, Natalia, author. | Stockman, Beryl, translator. | Ginzburg,
Natalia. Famiglia. English. | Ginzburg, Natalia. Borghesia. English. | Gudas,
Eric, writer of afterword.
Title: Family and borghesia : two novellas / by Natalia Ginzburg ; translated by
Beryl Stockman ; afterword by Eric Gudas.
Description: New York City : New York Review Books, [2021] | Series: New
York Review Books classics
Identifiers: LCCN 2020013641 (print) | LCCN 2020013642 (ebook) | ISBN
9781681375083 (paperback) | ISBN 9781681375090 (ebook)
Subjects: LCSH: Ginzburg, Natalia—Translations into English.
Classification: LCC PQ4817.I5 A2 2021 (print) | LCC PQ4817.I5 (ebook) |
DDC 853/.912—dc23
LC record available at https://lccn.loc.gov/2020013641
LC ebook record available at https://lccn.loc.gov/2020013642

ISBN 978-1-68137-508-3
Available as an electronic book; ISBN 978-1-68137-509-0

Printed in the United States of America on acid-free paper.
10 9 8 7 6 5 4 3 2

CONTENTS

FAMILY

A MAN and a woman went to see a film one summer Sunday afternoon. With them were a young girl of about fourteen and two boys of about seven. The man was tall and handsome with black hair, a large dark-skinned face and a large mouth set in a serious line. He wore black glasses and a crumpled blue suit. The woman, who was short and not very good-looking, had a tiny face and an olive complexion. Her black hair was twisted into a tight knot on top of her head. She had a long thin nose, green eyes and bushy eyebrows, sloping shoulders and broad hips. She wore a denim skirt and a blue T-shirt faded almost white. The two were friends and had known each other many years. When they were young they had lived together for a while, as lovers, but now they were just friends. The girl, who was called Angelica, was the woman's daughter. She was tall, with flaming red hair that fell about her shoulders, and a tuft over her forehead that completely hid one of her yellowy-brown eyes. She was covered in freckles. She wore a full grass-green skirt and a raw silk blouse. The smaller of the two boys was the man's son. His name was Piergiorgio, but everyone called him Dodò. He was fat, with straight chestnut hair combed forward and round, shy eyes. A camel-hair jumper was tied round his waist. The other boy was thin and dark and had big, white, prominent teeth. He was the child of one of the neighbours, a woman called Isa Meli. She was tired that day and wanted to spend the whole afternoon sleeping. 'Why has he got that jumper?' said Angelica, pointing to the fat little boy. She had a thin, severe, matter-of-fact voice. She was most displeased at having to go out on a Sunday afternoon with her mother and with those two children, and her one eye, peering out from amongst the freckles, wore a stern, bored expression. The man pushed the tuft of hair back from her temple, and for a split second, her other eye appeared. Then the tuft of hair hid it again. 'Because sometimes when you go to an air-conditioned cinema', said the man, 'it's like the North Pole.'

The film, which was in colour, was called *Abyss*. It was about millionaires in a gleaming white villa on a lonely beach, drinking fizzy drinks, swimming, sunbathing and quarrelling over an inheritance. The man and the woman were not following the story, they were both engrossed in their own affairs. The man was thinking about a letter his wife had written him the day before, from Venice. He was carrying it in his jacket pocket. She had been in Venice for more than a month now. This year, for the first time in his life, Dodò had not been taken to the seaside for his holidays. He just spent the mornings in Fregene, and the afternoons at home, getting bored. The man did not love his wife any more, but he was jealous. He kept thinking she must have someone in Venice and mentally scrutinizing the list of people who were there with her. He found himself doing this many times during the course of each day, in fact, and the whole process was humiliating. He could have taken Dodò on holiday himself perhaps, but he had not the slightest wish to, and told himself by way of an excuse that he must finish the book he was writing, on the suburbs of modern towns and cities. The woman was thinking about her parents. She and Angelica always went to dinner with them on Sundays, and, every week, she would end up arguing with them about politics. They had grown so reactionary of late. Daniele, the thin little boy, was laughing, even though *Abyss* was not in the least bit funny. He was laughing and wriggling about and swinging his legs and shaking Dodò who was sitting next to him. Dodò was laughing too, looking up at his father with round, frightened eyes. The air-conditioning must have been out of order, because there was no humming noise and it was as hot in there as outside. 'North Pole indeed,' said Angelica. The man said he thought there was a cartoon film on at another cinema nearby, which would be more suitable for children, and the air-conditioning there was normally in excellent working order. The woman asked him why he had not said so before. He said he had meant to but she had seemed so keen to see *Abyss*. She said that cartoons really were more than she could bear, but if they wanted to go and see them, she would wait for them outside in a café. Angelica said they were mad; they had paid five thousand lire for the tickets. Someone in the row behind went shh! The millionaires were in a speedboat, ploughing through a swirling blue sea, throwing spray high in the air all around them. They died one by one, some of them killed by each other and the rest eaten by a shark. It was still afternoon when they came out of the cinema. The man felt as if his head was full of sea, sand, fizzy drinks, sharks and gushing blood.

They went to a pavement café by the side of a small square. A waiter suggested they try the gypsy sundae, and Angelica and the two boys said that was all right. The man and the woman both ordered beers. The gypsy sundae came in a tall glass, with a mountain of whipped cream, topped by three glacé cherries, some pistachio nuts, and with a wafer stuck right in the middle. The man finished his beer and wiped his mouth, forehead and hands with his handkerchief. The woman asked him why he was so gloomy. He said he had had a nasty letter from Ninetta. Ninetta was his wife, Dodò's mother. 'What sort of nasty?' asked the woman. 'Petty and spiteful,' said the man. Ninetta was absolutely detestable in the woman's eyes. They thought about her, each in their different way. The man pictured her before him, tall and delicate-looking, with thin, slightly rounded shoulders and a long neck, her face framed in a soft, black fringe of hair. She had a milk-white complexion and a smile which she offered in the way that you would hold out a precious object. He did not love her, but he saw that black fringe before his eyes every moment of the day, and it was humiliating to see it there and suffer, not out of love, but out of feelings of irritation and the accumulation of years of grim, unhappy resentment. The woman thought Ninetta was as stupid as a pear. Strange she should have written a letter, said the man. It was not like her at all, she usually preferred to phone. She had not said when she intended to come home, either in the letter or by phone. Dodò was being looked after by a Spanish au pair girl, who was beautiful and totally useless because she had loads of money and boyfriends and was always going out. Fortunately, though, there was Evelina. Evelina came every day, took Dodò to Fregene then brought him back and stayed with him all afternoon. The caretaker's wife was cooking for them because Ninetta had quarrelled with the cook and sacked her just before she went away to Venice. Evelina thought she had done the right thing, because the cook was dirty. 'I can't remember who Evelina is,' said Angelica. Evelina was Ninetta's mother, Dodò's grandmother. 'I'd be lost without Evelina,' said the man, adding, however, that she was a terrible fusspot. She would have fainted if she had seen Dodò eating the gypsy sundae. She disapproved of whipped cream and pistachio nuts and glacé cherries. She saw artificial colouring everywhere. 'There's no colouring in whipped cream,' said Angelica. 'No, but there must be something else that's not right, like dirty milk or dirty sugar, something of the sort,' said the man, and added under his breath that, actually, Evelina was a frightful bore. She took Dodò to Fregene, but not to the beach. They spent the mornings with some friends of hers, in a villa with a swimming-pool. She was enough to bore you to death with that swimming-pool. According to her, the water was so clear and clean you could drink it. Dodò said they had a beautiful little white dog there called Snowflake. But no other children for you to play with, said the man. No, said Dodò, no other children. The caretaker's son had been there twice, no, three times but then he had gone away again almost at once. Dodò was eating the gypsy sundae very slowly. Daniele had finished his and was inside the café watching the table football. 'We'll still be here at midnight,' said

Angelica, 'you wait and see.' 'What's the hurry?' said the man. 'There's nobody after us. Besides, it's nice here, and it's starting to get cooler now.' The woman stroked Dodò's hair. It was fair, straight and fine. She drew a comb out of her straw bag and started to make a parting at the front. The man told her to stop it. Dodò's hair did not need combing. Anyway, he did not like him with a parting, he preferred him with a fringe, like his mother. What really needed combing was that tuft of Angelica's. He took the comb away from the woman and started on the offending tuft. Angelica moved her head aside and gave him a slap on the hand. Cute, said the man. There were such things as hair-grips and slides, he said, and they were excellent for keeping hair in place. You could even buy them at a tobacconist's.

The man's name was Carmine Donati and he was forty years old. He was an architect. He earned good money at his work, but had not achieved any of the goals he had set himself in his youth. The book he was writing on the suburbs of modern towns and cities seemed mediocre to him one moment, and fresh and original the next. The woman's name was Ivana Riviera and she was thirty-seven. She made her living from translations, and was looking for a full-time job, but could not find one. Many years before, when they were lovers and lived together, they had argued constantly about everything and tried to change one another. She wanted him to be freer. He thought she was untidy in the way she organized her time and kept house, and in her ideas. They used to wake up in the night and start arguing, and discussing each other's faults and wonder aloud whether they should get married or not. They had a tiny flat in via Casilina. It was more or less a single room, but there was a shower and a minute entrance hall. They cooked and slept in the same room. There was also a large terrace where they tried to grow flowers. They had an owl, a rabbit and a cat. The cat was called Fidel. Once, his parents came to stay with them. They were peasants from Vinchiaturo, a small village in the Abbruzzo. Ivana tried hard to be nice to them. It felt so strange to her, to be living with a man whose mother was almost illiterate and wore a black headscarf and had broken, black teeth. In turn, his parents were appalled and upset by the untidiness of the house, the rabbit, the owl and everything. They had plenty of rabbits of their own, but they gave them grass to eat. This rabbit was fed on dessert apples and specially cooked broccoli. Furthermore, they were absolutely unable to tolerate the idea of the two of them living together without being married, and they did not understand the reason why. Ivana's parents were both in America at the time. Her father was a mathematician and had been sent over there to teach courses in several universities. The letters they wrote her were full of mistrust. They were afraid this Carmine Donati, whom they had never met, might be no good. They knew he came from a poor family, and they did not mind that, but the idea that his mother was almost illiterate was too much for them to take. They thought maybe he was living with her for self-interested reasons, because he wanted to improve his social status. But when she wrote and told them she was pregnant, they wrote back and said they must get married. They had a baby girl, and called her Carmela, after his mother. They decided they would get married but put it off until spring, so that they could invite all their friends and have a big party on the terrace. The rabbit died, and they gave the owl away because the baby was frightened of it. But they still had the cat. Spring passed, and then summer, and they still had not got married because he was a little in love with a woman they always met at the restaurant. She was a photographer. The baby's birth certificate was in her mother's name, Riviera, and said father unknown. They did not argue during the night any more, partly so as not to wake the baby, but partly because it bored them terribly now to exchange thoughts of any kind. They hardly ever saw each other during the day, because he was working long hours in an office he shared, in via della Vite, and, as her parents were back from America, she always took the baby to their house, where there was a cool, shady terrace, surrounded by trees, much better than the one in via Casilina. The baby died of infantile paralysis when she was one and a half years old. After her death, they separated. Ivana never wanted to go back to the flat in via Casilina, not even to collect her winter clothes, so she sent her father to collect them instead. Carmine stayed there for a few more years, with Fidel the cat and a new girlfriend, not the photographer, an actress this time. Fidel disappeared over the roof-tops one night, and after that Carmine kept a large dog. But the dog insisted on sleeping on the bed at night, and his girlfriend would not tolerate that. Ivana eventually found living with her parents unbearable, and went to England, where she did a sculpture course. After that she took a job as an interpreter with a tourist agency, and then she worked as a cloakroom attendant in a home for the blind. She had her daughter Angelica by a Jewish glottology student she met at a party, a tall, lean boy with red hair. She did not love him, but wanted to have a baby. His name was Joachim Halevy. He took her to Bristol to meet his aunt, a gentle, white-haired woman who taught drawing in a kindergarten. He never knew he was a father, because, shortly after they met, he was taken into a psychiatric hospital. His aunt came all the way from Bristol to London to see Angelica, in the hospital where she was born. She came again when Ivana took Angelica back to Italy. She accompanied her to the train and gave Angelica a locket with a portrait of Joachim as a baby. Angelica was only four months old then. She wrote to them from time to time, and sent Angelica paper flowers to cut out every Christmas. News of Joachim was bad. When Ivana got back to Rome, she took a flat in via del Vantaggio. Her father and mother helped her out. They were tender and loving towards Angelica, bitter towards her. Her memory of Joachim was hazy, but somewhat painful. Sometimes, in her innermost thoughts, she would see his face, his leanness, the corduroy trousers he used to wear, his slouch. Occasionally she looked at the locket, and inside was his picture, a pink baby face against a sky-blue background. He used to beat her. Their relationship only lasted a few weeks, but, at the end of it, she locked herself in her room at the boarding-house until some mutual friends told her he had been taken into hospital. She still woke up in terror sometimes, in the middle of the night. Suppose he escaped from the hospital; he might come to Rome and try and move in with her and the baby in via del Vantaggio. However, she knew her fears were absurd, because, from what his aunt said, he had lost all will and memory. He could not even speak. He lay at the back of the ward like a limp rag. She met Carmine again, one evening, in the home of some mutual friends. He kissed her on both cheeks. They had not seen each other for ten years. He had spent several years in America, living on student grants, then had come back to Italy and got married. His wife, Ninetta, was with him. She was a tall, delicate-looking woman enveloped in a black shawl. She moved in a languid sort of way, as if she felt cold all the time, and sat on the floor on a pile of cushions playing with her long necklaces and then with the fringe of her shawl. Her big, pale blue, trusting eyes seemed to beg protection, and she offered her smile as if it were a precious jewel. Carmine said they must go. Ninetta had to feed Dodò. She was a marvellous wet nurse, he said, and added that they had time to see Ivana home though. They went on foot, because via del Vantaggio was very close by. Carmine and Ninetta lived in via Barnaba Oriani, which was in another area altogether. Carmine talked about nothing but his son all the way, and Ivana was bored. It is so boring to hear about babies when you have none of your own. Angelica was quite big now, and going to school. Ninetta, dressed in her fur coat, and with her shawl wrapped around her head, said nothing, just offered her smile. Ivana thought to herself that when they had had their baby, he had taken very little notice. He had scarcely looked at her. He had busied himself preparing the cradle just before she was born, and it had been a pretty cradle, a basket, with a pattern of little red flowers on the lining material. But after that, he had taken very little interest in the child. Perhaps he had been too young. Ivana

invited them to come upstairs for a moment, but they said
they had to go because Ninetta had to feed Dodò, and because
they had guests. Dodò had just cut his first tooth and Carmine's parents had come up from Vinchiaturo to celebrate.
The next day, he phoned and apologized for not having asked
about her at all. He said he had done all the talking, but really
he was dying to know if she was well, if she was working, if
she was happy. He had heard she had a daughter and that
made him very happy. He asked if he could come and see her.
He came on his own. He said Ninetta had taken a great liking
to her and had asked him a lot of things about her on the way
home. She wanted her to come to dinner with them and see
the house and the baby. She had a slight sore throat at the
moment, but they would arrange it soon. He said it might be
better to wait until the guests, his parents that was, had gone
home. He asked her if she remembered them. She did remember them. He said they were absolutely enchanted by the baby.
They spent hours gazing at him as he lay in his cot, talking
about his eyes and hands and feet and admiring them. So the
baby had a cot, not a cradle said Ivana, inquiringly. That's
right, said Carmine, a cot with wooden railings you can take
out and use as a playpen. He's been sleeping in it ever since
he was born. No one uses cradles any more. His parents were
enchanted by the house and by Ninetta, who was absolutely
delightful with them. She noted the adjective 'delightful'. It
was a word that was not him, he would never have used it at
one time. He said his mother had taught Ninetta how to make
hundreds of things: home-made pasta, aubergines in oil. Ivana
was finding him boring. She could not care less about aubergines in oil or the sweet nothings Ninetta and his mother
exchanged between them. She told him on the phone a few
days later that he had become extremely boring. 'I don't care
a fuck about aubergines in oil,' she said, and went on to say
she could not understand why that child of theirs was called
Dodò. She thought it was horrible to call children by pet
names and nicknames, Dodò, Fufu, Pupu. What a horrible,
irritating affected habit! He got offended and told her she hadn't

become boring because she had always been extremely boring anyway, and scatty and full of screwy ideas. Nevertheless, he came round to see her immediately afterwards. He had bought a roast chicken from a take-away in via del Babuino. Angelica was already in bed, but they got her up, and she sat at the kitchen table in her pink flannel nightdress and shared the chicken with them. Angelica and Ivana had had supper really, but they usually only had milky coffee and bread and butter. Carmine got into the habit of coming quite often. Ivana sat and worked at her translations, and he sometimes looked up words in the dictionary for her while he played chess with Angelica or lay on the settee and read the paper. About midnight, he would phone Ninetta to say he was coming home soon. Ninetta would send a big kiss to Ivana and Angelica. But he would still stay stretched out on the sofa for a while, reading, smoking and looking out of the window at the trees along the road, the bridge, the river and the roof-tops bathed in moonlight. When they were alone, they usually talked about the present: Ninetta, Angelica and Dodò. They rarely talked of the time when they had lived together. To both of them it seemed like a strange, remote era when they had got the absurd idea into their heads that they could live together, even though they were so different and had opposite and irreconcilable characters. They sometimes remembered Fidel, the cat, with affection, but they never spoke of their dead daughter.

At last the dinner in the via Barnaba Oriani was arranged, or rather, a supper. But a long time had passed since Ivana and Carmine had met again at their friends' house, and Dodò was now nearly three years old. Ninetta and Ivana hardly ever saw each other. Once or twice, Ninetta had been to via del Vantaggio, and once or twice, Carmine, Ninetta and Ivana had been out together for an evening. One day, Ninetta phoned Ivana and begged her to come because she was alone in the house with Dodò and he was very ill. He had a temperature of a hundred and two, and she could not find Carmine. She did not know where he was. She could not find her mother, or the pediatrician. She had not even been able to find

Ciaccia Oppi, who was a dear neighbour of theirs and knew everything there was to know about children. She was so worried, she said. Ivana took a taxi and went to via Oriani, where she had never been before. But by that time the paediatrician had arrived, and so had Ciaccia Oppi, and Ninetta's worries had completely vanished because the paediatrician had said it was only a cold. As it was pouring with rain and there were no taxis available, Ciaccia Oppi gave Ivana a lift home. The car got stuck in a traffic-jam for over three-quarters of an hour, and Ivana had to make conversation with Ciaccia Oppi, who seemed to her to be an absolute twit. After a while, they had nothing more to say to each other, and they were stuck there, in silence, with the rain beating down on the roof. Then the car refused to start because of the rain, and Ivana and Ciaccia Oppi had to push it for some distance. That evening, Ninetta and Carmine phoned to apologize. They had heard from Ciaccia Oppi that she had had to walk home in the rain in the end. They invited her to supper the following evening. Ciaccia Oppi would be there too. She had taken a great liking to her. Ivana said she found her quite nice, perhaps, but an absolute twit. Ninetta said Ciaccia Oppi gave the impression of being silly, but she was not really, she was extremely cultured and read an awful lot and knew all sorts of things. The guests at the supper were Ciaccia Oppi and her husband, who was a doctor specializing in diseases of the metabolism, another married couple, both architects, and Ninetta's little sister, who had been invited to keep Angelica company. Angelica had decided at the last minute, however, that she would rather stay at home. Ivana did not like the house in via Barnaba Oriani one bit, and said so, having decided a long time ago that she never wanted to tell even the tiniest of lies. There were red curtains in the living-room, because Ninetta and Carmine both adored that colour. The settee was red too, so were the carpets and the table-cloth, and the waiter who served at table was wearing a red jacket. Ivana said she felt like something out of the last scene of *Rosemary's Baby* where everything was the colour of blood. Next to the settee was a lamp with a furry white paper shade. Ivana said it looked like a silkworm. Dangling from the ceiling, above the table, was a long, smooth, white paper lampshade. She said it looked like a contraceptive. The two comparisons were not appreciated. Nobody smiled. Only Ninetta's smile remained fixed and radiant. As soon as the meal was over, Ninetta's little sister left, so did the waiter, since he was employed by her mother, who lived downstairs. When they had gone, Carmine said he hoped neither of them had heard the word 'contraceptive', and that the matter would not be mentioned downstairs. They were most particular downstairs about the words they used. In fact, Evelina was very particular altogether. When she lent them her waiter, she always issued a thousand don'ts. Don't tire him, don't spoil him, don't give him too much to eat or too little, don't use vulgar words or make unconventional remarks in his presence. According to her, unconventional remarks were a bad influence on waiters, they were a source of confusion and only encouraged them to snigger in the kitchen. ' "Evelina," stop saying "Evelina," ' said Ninetta. 'You've got a way of saying my mother's name as if you were making fun of her, and I don't like it.' Her smile was fixed and radiant, but her voice was acrimonious. At last, a discussion broke out between Ivana and the two architects, about politics, and Ivana called them both reactionaries. Ciaccia Oppi's husband agreed with her, and as she thought he was a total imbecile, this irritated her. Ninetta also agreed with her, and this irritated her too. She suddenly took sides with the architects. By the time the evening was over, Carmine was extremely tired, and felt that he disliked all of them, the two architects, the Oppis, Ninetta and Ivana. Ivana because she always replied so abruptly whenever Ninetta dared to say anything, and Ninetta because she frowned and pretended to listen intently, when he was sure she was really thinking the most trivial, banal thoughts, such as what to do with the left-over risotto, and was it possible to salvage the courgette mould, which had not turned out well and consequently no one had eaten much of it? Perhaps she could put it back together again and serve it to some cousins of hers who were coming to visit and who were not too fussy. In the hall, when everyone was ready to go, Ivana and the architects were still arguing loudly enough to wake Dodò. After they had finally gone, Ivana's voice could still be heard echoing up from the street. 'God, what a voice,' said Ninetta, as she sat down underneath the silkworm to write in her diary what they had eaten for supper and who had been there. She always did this, so as not to serve the same dishes to the same people twice. However, after she had written 'courgette mould' an immense feeling of melancholy came over her, and she told Carmine to get those horrendous leftovers out of her sight immediately. While he was clearing the table, she shut her diary and threw it down on to the carpet noisily. She looked in the mirror opposite the settee, and studied her face as she always did, with the liveliest of interest. She touched her cheeks and lips and ruffled up her soft, black fringe. Then she and Carmine began to quarrel for no particular reason, because there was no mineral water left, because there was barely any heat coming from the radiators, because Dodò had woken up and wanted the rag monkey he always took to bed with him, and it was not easy to find. In the end, she threw herself into bed in tears and told Carmine he had been horrible to her all evening and had looked at her as if she was a silly goose; as if she was a complete stranger to him rather than his wife. The architects were horrible too, Ciaccia Oppi must have been bored to death. Everything was boring and horrible. She did not say a word about Ivana. She had written in her diary that she never wanted to invite that woman Ivana to supper again because she treated her like a silly goose. She was cold and huddled into the quilt, shaking with sobs. Carmine bent down to console the black fringe as it lay on the pillow.

Next day, Ninetta said to Carmine that, of course, everyone knew Ivana had a lot of men and was always changing them. There was Matteo Tramonti, for example, a twenty-year-old who played the guitar. Ciaccia Oppi had some friends who went regularly to a small theatre near Piazzale Flaminio, where he played and sang. Another of Ivana's men was a doctor called Amos Elia. He lived in a village near Todi, called Fontechiusa. Ivana often went to see him, but sometimes she had to wait for hours in a bar in the central square in Todi, because he had a lot of patients and was very busy, and was rather indifferent towards her anyway. Ciaccia Oppi had told her that too. She had a cousin who lived in Todi. Carmine said it was true. Ivana had had a relationship with this doctor, Amos Elia, for several years, but it had brought her no happiness at all, and it was true he was indifferent to her because of a sort of innate bitterness, and because he had very little interest in life. Ninetta said Ivana had an ugly long nose and a stale complexion, and she always wore the most horrible clothes. Carmine said maybe this was true. But she had no other men. Amos Elia was the only one, and she rarely saw him, because he suffered from long periods of depression that lasted for months at a time, and he did not always want to see her. As for Matteo Tramonti, she used to invite him to stay once in a while, because he had a rather difficult, complicated relationship with his mother. She was a lawyer, a tall woman with white hair and a limp, who had a deep guttural voice and said *w* instead of *r*. Matteo Tramonti was a homosexual. He was eighteen years old, short and thickset, with a short, sparse, downy beard. He too had a guttural voice and said *w* instead of *r* like his mother. Sometimes he stayed at his mother's, a flat in Piazza Adriana, other times in a commune in via del Boschetto, and when he was tired of his mother's and the commune, he would come and plant himself in Ivana's flat. He slept on a camp-bed in a spare room at the far end of the hall, and they could hear him shuffling about in his slippers late into the night. Angelica used to call him 'a damned cretin', because all that nervous shuffling kept her awake, and he used to reply, 'you'we a vipew'. In the morning, he would say to Ivana, 'youw daughtew's a little vipew, she's always huwling abuse at me.' While drinking his morning cup of coffee in the kitchen with Angelica, he would tell her off because when he pushed aside the hair from her neck, he found her neck was slightly dirty. 'A giwl who doesn't wash pwopewly is a weal disgwace,' he always used to say. Angelica always replied promptly that, since he was a poof, he wouldn't know about girls anyway. And besides, he didn't wash either. He would then explain that he was, however, extremely clean by nature, and never sweated and had no body odours. Meanwhile, his mother would phone to find out, 'what sowt of mood hew boy was in', and Ivana, huddled in the chair, still in her night-dress, would hear that slow, guttural voice on the other end of the telephone line relating remote episodes of her son's childhood and adolescence. Normally, Ivana was not very patient with people, but for some reason she was extremely patient with Signora Tramonti. However, that might have been because Amos Elia had introduced her to Matteo Tramonti, so perhaps she saw the boy and even the fat lady lawyer in a special light. Ninetta said she was sick of all these stories of late nights and early mornings, and she was not in the least bit curious to know about Ivana's private life.

All Carmine knew of Amos Elia was a grey, woollen, cable-patterned jumper and a pale lilac acrylic scarf which had been left lying on top of the chest of drawers in via del Vantaggio. He had lent them both to Ivana last time she had been to see him at Fontechiusa. It had been a very windy day, and he had thought she was not dressed sensibly. Ivana said she was going to take them back to him soon, when she went to see him again, but she did not know when that would be, because he had told her over the phone that he did not want to see her at the moment; he was too depressed. Ivana rarely spoke of Amos Elia, and when she did, she said very little. They had met one summer, when Angelica was small, and she and Ivana were spending their summer holidays in Todi. He lived alone and was poor. He charged his patients very little. He loved music and spent what money he had on records. He had a house, which was inherited from his family. It was big, dirty and bare. He also had a dog. Matteo Tramonti told Carmine that Amos Elia was 'incwedible, weally incwedible'. He had been known to phone Ivana and say he wanted to see her right away, and she had jumped in her car early in the morning, while it was still dark. Then she had had to wait all day for him in the bar in Todi, and when he had finally appeared, he had told her he could only spend quarter of an hour with her. He did not always take her to his house, because sometimes his brother and sister-in-law stayed with him, and he kept Ivana well hidden from them, thinking they would not like each other at all. He was very intelligent, said Matteo Tramonti, but 'stwange and quite incwedible'. Sometimes, when he and Ivana had not seen each other for months, he would come into the bar with that tired walk of his, hold out his hand half-heartedly, sit down, rub his eyes and yawn. He was a great yawner. Then all he could find to say to her was, 'I'm glad you'we hewe, I am glad you'we hewe', then maybe something like, 'Mothew of God, what a dweadful jacket you'we weawing, you look like something the cat dwagged in.' As for him, he would be wearing a coat that looked as if his dog slept on it, and it probably did. 'He's obviously tired of her then,' said Carmine. 'Faw fwom it,' said Matteo Tramonti. 'He's vewy fond of hew in his own way. Sometimes he gets despewate and calls hew. He likes to make hew come and then pwetend he doesn't cawe a fuck about hew. He weally makes hew suffew poow giwl.' Carmine and Matteo Tramonti had become friends, and they used to leave Ivana's house together and walk along the bank of the Tiber or go and have a cappuccino at Canova's. Once they bumped into Ninetta there, with Ciaccia Oppi, a group of painters and a few other people. Matteo Tramonti fled, muttering to Carmine that he had seen that woman dressed up like a sheep before, and he could not stand her. That woman dressed up like a sheep was Ciaccia Oppi, who was wearing a big, white, shaggy fur coat that evening.

One evening, some time later, towards the end of winter, at about midnight, Carmine and Ninetta were already asleep when the phone rang. Carmine answered it. It was Matteo Tramonti. Something dreadful had happened, he said. Amos Elia had killed himself with phenobarbital. He did not have the courage to go and tell Ivana, and begged Carmine to go with him. Carmine told Ninetta, 'Amos Elia is dead,' and started to get dressed in a great hurry. Ninetta followed him around the room barefoot, her scanty, green voile nightdress a flutter, repeating 'Amos Elia, who's Amos Elia?' over and over. Carmine told her hurriedly that he was a doctor, a friend of Ivana's, and also a friend of Matteo Tramonti. How could she possibly have forgotten, they had talked about him often enough, but anyway, he must fly now. He said he was taking the big car because they might all have to go to Todi, and Ninetta said but her mother and Uncle Mimmo and Aunt Pina needed the big car next day, they had to go to Lucca. 'Never mind,' he said, 'I'm taking it anyway.' Ninetta nodded her agreement. She was sitting on the sofa in the hall now, rubbing her long bare legs, saying 'All who, all who have got to go to Todi?' He buttoned up his raincoat, and as he went down in the lift, he thought about her sitting there in that scanty nightdress, her big, delicate white breasts bursting out of the tulle, her fringe quite still and her eyes full of bewilderment as she kept repeating, 'All who?'

Matteo Tramonti was waiting for him in the piazza del Popolo, and he had a friend with him, a blond boy called Giuliano Grimaglia. Carmine had seen them together before. Matteo Tramonti said he had been staying at his mother's that evening, and someone from Todi had phoned him, a boy he knew very well. He worked at a petrol station. Amos Elia had cured him of nephritis. He was sobbing into the telephone, and at first, Matteo had not been able to make out what was happening. 'When I finally undewstood,' he said, 'I was just. Well, I didn't weally think he would do it. He was always thweatening to, but I nevew thought he weally would. It was with phenobawbital. I saw him a month ago, he came hewe to Wome. He didn't want to see Ivana. He told me not to tell hew he was hewe. He said, "I don't want to see that woman the cat dwagged in, I don't feel stwong enough to cope with hew this time." He was so intelligent. He was absolutely extwaodinawy. He cuwed people, he wanted them to live, and yet he hated people and hated life. He was so stwange and so full of contwadictions. The whole thing's incwedible, just too too incwedible.' He said Ivana already knew. She had phoned him and was waiting for them. The blond boy went away. When they got to Ivana's, Isa Meli was there. Isa Meli was a slender woman with black hair falling loose about her shoulders. She lived in the flat next door. She was separated from her husband, and taught in a middle school. She was doing the washing-up with the help of Angelica and her own two daughters, who were about Angelica's age. That way, she said, Ivana could go without having to worry about the dishes. Isa Meli's youngest child, Daniele, was asleep on a sofa in the living room. Isa Meli said they had been having supper with Ivana that evening, and at one point there had been a phone call from Todi. It was the sister of the man who owned the bar where Ivana always used to wait for Amos Elia. That was how Ivana had found out about the tragedy. Ivana was sitting in the corner of the kitchen with her coat on, ready to go, and when Carmine and Matteo Tramonti bent down to give her a hug, she just nodded her head.

They reached Fontechiusa just before dawn. It was a tiny village, no more than a group of houses on the brow of a hill. Amos Elia's house overlooked the square, and had a long balcony with rusty railings, adorned by a withered climbing wistaria. It had remained a sort of faded pink colour, despite the fact that the houses all around had recently been painted cherry-red, or apricot. The entrance hall was long and dark with a tiled floor. At the far end was the room where he lay, dressed in a double-breasted jacket and a big red silk tie. The jacket smelled of mothballs. He was a small man with bristly grey hair, a wispy grey beard and a small, stern mouth with thin, tightly pressed lips. The room was full of people. There were women crying and women praying. Carmine had lived in the country as a child, and the people in that room were all familiar figures to him, the women with their black head-scarves, the faces all pitted and dried out by the sun and the wind and covered in fine wrinkles. He was familiar too, with the worn-out terracotta tiles on the floor, and the brazier and the smell of ashes and mould. He had lived in a house very similar to this one until he was twelve years old, then some uncles had taken him away and placed him in a boarding-school to study. His parents still lived in rooms very similar to these, and although he sent them money, they never did much to change them. There was nothing but the four bare walls of the room and a bed. However, the kitchen, where they went next, was completely different. It was nothing like a traditional country kitchen. It was littered with medical journals, newspapers and atlases, empty bottles covered in dust, old woollens and tins of food. Carmine was introduced to Amos Elia's brother and sister-in-law. His brother was small, dishevelled and frail looking. His sister-in-law had a huge head of blonde curls and a face like a doll. He was called Armandino and she was called Ornella. He had an electrical shop in Viterbo. Matteo Tramonti whispered to Carmine that he was going for a walk in the square with Ivana, because she could not stand those two. Carmine stayed behind, trapped between Ornella and Armandino. They thought he was an old friend of Amos Elia's, and he felt it was too complicated to explain that he had never seen him before. They wanted him to have a cup of coffee with them. They said Amos had left two notes. They were not addressed to anybody. One said: 'The dog mustn't be moved away from the village.' The other said: 'You must inform my wife. I expect she's in a terrible state financially. Send her the money as soon as you've sold the house. Her name is Irene Kramer and she lives in West Berlin. She's moved and I don't know her address. She might even be dead, of course.' Armandino knew very little about this wife of Amos's. She was half Russian, half Belgian. She was also half Jewish. She was half everything. He had only seen her once, at Viterbo, many years ago. She could not speak Italian and had a very faint voice. Amos used to talk to her in his own brand of French. They had only lived together for a few months. There was still a coat of hers hanging in a wardrobe in the hall. Armandino was wondering how he could trace her. How he could find out whether she was alive or dead? Yes, of course, through the Consulate, but he did not know anyone at the Consulate. Carmine thought Evelina might have a few acquaintances at the consulates and embassies. He promised to see what he could do, and gave Armandino his phone number. As they were going through the hall, Ornella wanted to show him the coat. It was hanging in the wardrobe. There was nothing else hanging in there, just piles of blankets and still more newspapers. It was a black coat with a big, threadbare, astrakhan collar. It looked like something the cat had dragged in.

Armandino said there was something else worrying him too. The mayor did not want the dog. They would have to give it to someone else, but the note said, 'the dog mustn't be moved from the village', so it would not be a good idea even to take it to Viterbo. The dog was outside at the back of the house, and they wanted him to see it. Outside the back door of the house was a big tree and a pile of rubbish. The dog was tied to the tree. It was just an old dog, long and lean, with long droopy ears and a sad expression. Armando said it was called Sheriff.

Armandino and Ornella had attached themselves to Carmine. They followed him across the square and into the tobacconist's, where he had said he was going, in order to get rid of them. The tobacconist's was also the bar, and Matteo Tramonti and Ivana were in there drinking cappuccino. Armandino invited them all to dinner, saying there was an excellent restaurant out in the countryside not far away, where they served a very good wine. Ivana replied that the cappuccino was enough for her. They extricated themselves with difficulty, Ivana walking hurriedly towards the car with her hands in her pockets, and Carmine and Matteo Tramonti promising to come back soon.

They spent the whole afternoon walking in the countryside. Carmine kept his arm around Ivana's shoulders. She did not speak. She did not cry. He remembered that she had not even cried when the baby died. He looked at her pale profile as they walked, her long, thin, sharp nose, her brown hair twisted into a knot on top of her head, her shabby, worn-out jacket that looked like something the cat had dragged in. None of them spoke. Carmine thought to himself that these two, Ivana and Matteo Tramonti, were the people with whom he felt best in the world. It was easy to be with them. When he was with anyone else, such as Ninetta, and Ninetta's various friends and relatives, or even the architects who worked with him at the studio, he felt forced to adopt a stiff, complicated stance, and he felt himself become numb and cramped.

Then, suddenly, while they were sitting resting in a meadow, Ivana and Matteo Tramonti started talking about Amos Elia, gaily, as if he were still alive. The times when he sang. When he cooked minestrone. When he told them about certain dreams he used to have which were long and strange and full of animals. When he used to dress up in his double-breasted blue jacket and silk tie and go to supper at the mayor's house. The way he used to ride his motor bike so cautiously and nervously, bumping up and down on the country mule-tracks. He had not used his motor bike for the last few years, and a man from the village looked after it for him. He used to go and visit it sometimes, in much the same way as you would go and see an animal or a child you had placed in some-one else's care. Sometimes he talked about his estranged wife. He had married her during the war. She was a foreigner and half Jewish. He had married her in order to improve her status with the authorities, and for no other reason. For a brief time, however, a few weeks or months, he had wanted to have a child with her, but he had soon realized this was a crazy idea. Besides, she had a prolapsed womb. He soon found out he could not stand her, she was so boring, or so he said. And yet, he had always kept certain of her belongings: a small ivory tortoise, a tattered manicure-set and the coat. He remembered her faint voice and her slow, restricted movements. He said it was because she had low blood-pressure and poor blood. After the war they had separated. She had only come back to see him in Fontechiusa once, and they had quarrelled terribly, about politics, because she was against Stalin, and so was he, but from a different point of view; and also because she had left a woollen vest in the kitchen and he had inadvertently used it to clean his motor bike. She had left in great indignation that day, burning with indignation, in fact, in a feeble sort of way. There were red spots on her normally pallid cheeks. He had seen her off on the bus with a great sigh of relief, and placed a parcel of nourishing food on her lap for the journey, while she kept repeating that he treated her things as if they were old rags. However, she had forgotten to take her coat, and had written to him later telling him not to bother sending it, because he was incapable of making up a parcel, and he was incapable of buying food too, because the cheese in that food pack had tasted like soap. After that she had disappeared, and he had lost all trace of her. She was not much of a woman anyway, he said, and besides, he liked living alone. He was very attached to his brother, and tolerated his sister-in-law, although he used to tease her about her blonde curls and her sling-back shoes, and he got really angry every time he saw her put on an apron and start cleaning his house. He did not want anyone cleaning his house for him. Towards evening, it poured with rain, and they were soaked to the bone when they arrived at the hotel in Todi, where they had booked rooms. They decided to have supper in the hotel restaurant and spent a long time in the foyer afterwards, drinking grappa and drying their clothes by a wood stove.

They left for home next day, after the funeral. Carmine said he wanted to pay the hotel bill, because Ivana was poor and Matteo Tramonti was only a boy. Ivana protested a bit. She pointed out that she was not all that poor, her parents were well-off and gave her money whenever she needed it. Matteo Tramonti did not protest. They had been driving for half an hour when Ivana said she wanted to go back and get the dog. She could not stop thinking about him still tied up in that dismal yard. 'You'we pwobably wight,' said Matteo Tramonti, 'what does he mean, the dog mustn't be moved fwom the village? Whyevew not? It's just one of those widiculous things he used to come out with evewy so often.' They turned back. Armandino and Ornella were in the kitchen of Amos's house, leafing through atlases, magazines and newspapers. Carmine went in alone. He said Signora Riviera would like to take the dog with her. Her daughter Angelica was crazy about dogs. This was a lie, because Angelica could not bear dogs. Armandino was doubtful about the idea. He still wanted to try and persuade the mayor. But Ornella said, really, one should read between the lines of a dead person's wishes. Amos wanted the dog to be happy, and what could be nicer for a dog than to be loved by a child. The dog was still there, tied to the tree. It was handed into the car to Matteo Tramonti. They set off, while Armandino and Ornella stood and watched, two little figures rooted to the spot. He was thin and stooping and she was plump and straight-backed. Matteo Tramonti said they looked as if they had stepped out of a children's nursery rhyme. Once upon a time, there were two people called Armandino and Ornella. Armandino was very good and Ornella was very beautiful. The dog barked all the way home. Ivana said perhaps it was because he was unhappy about being taken into town. 'Oh no,' said Matteo Tramonti, 'no wegwets, if you don't mind.'

Carmine got back to his house late in the afternoon. It was Sunday. Ninetta was wearing a new red jumper. Dodò was sitting on the floor playing with his toy cars. Evelina had brought a *foccaccia* and they were all drinking tea. Ciaccia Oppi was sewing. There was to be a fancy-dress party at her mother's villa in Velletri in a few days, and Ninetta had asked her to embroider a big half-moon on to a wizard's costume for Dodò. The whole room was dominated by Evelina's large head and gauzy blue hair, her tall, commanding, flourishing figure and her smile, which, like Ninetta, she offered as if it were a precious jewel. But behind it, there was also a sort of satisfaction at being so tall and straight and exuberant in her old age. Her presence was like a monument to elegant old age, healthy, shrewdly wealthy and wise. Carmine suddenly felt he detested her. He detested the two people with her as well. It seemed horrible to him that mixed up in all this hate was Dodò. He detested the whole room and all the people in it. He said he wanted to go for a walk with Dodò, but they dissuaded him. Dodò was about to have his semolina, and then he had to be fitted for his wizard's costume. 'You don't look sad, even though you have come back from a funeral,' said Evelina. 'You look annoyed about something rather than sad. You look as if you're angry with someone.' 'I'm tired,' said Carmine. 'But you don't look tired either. You've got some colour in your cheeks. You're usually much paler than that.' 'I love the countryside,' he said. 'I was born in the country, so I feel good when I'm in the country. It was beautiful where we've just been.' 'We, because there were obviously a lot of you since you took the big car. Pino, Mimmo and I had to cancel our trip to Lucca, but it doesn't matter, it wasn't important. We didn't take the mini because it isn't in very good condition. I'm sorry for Mimmo's sake, because he was so looking forward to the trip,' said Evelina. 'I'm sorry, forgive me,' said Carmine. 'Well, we know Ivana Riviera was there, because it was her friend who died, and who else was there?' enquired Evelina. 'Matteo Tramonti.' 'Ah, Matteo Tramonti, Signora Tramonti the lawyer's son, a boy with certain tendencies so they say.' 'You mean he's a poof, poor things,' said Ciaccia Oppi. 'It was such a beautiful place,' said Carmine. 'I'd have liked to be a country doctor like Amos Elia.' 'He liked it so much that he killed himself,' said Ninetta. 'Oh, but he was just a great big neurotic,' said Ciaccia Oppi. 'My cousin told me so. She comes from around there. He was all alone. He had no one, except a brother, perhaps.' 'He had his wife,' said Carmine. 'She's in Berlin. We ought to try and trace her through the consulates and embassies, if you have any contacts there.' 'He didn't have a wife,' said Ciaccia Oppi. 'Yes he did,' said Carmine. 'You didn't go to Oreste Padula's funeral even though you'd been to his house for dinner hundreds of times, and yet you rush off to the funeral of this doctor, whom you've never even seen before,' said Ninetta. 'And who's Oreste Padula?' asked Ciaccia Oppi. 'A relative of ours who died of thrombosis the other day,' said Ninetta. 'You've got so many relatives,' said Carmine. 'I can't keep track of all of them.' 'You've got swarms of relatives too,' said Ninetta, 'in Vinchiaturo and L'Aquila, and I'm nice to all of them. I write them postcards. I invite them here when they're in town, and they're not much fun either.' 'Amos Elia didn't have a wife,' said Ciaccia Oppi. 'Yes he did,' said Carmine, 'and we should look for her.' Evelina shook her blue head, slowly. 'I don't know any ambassadors in Berlin,' she said. 'That's nice,' said Ninetta. 'We've got to go running around after Amos Elia's wife now.'

Matteo Tramonti phoned Carmine that evening, after supper, and said Ivana was feeling very depressed and might be glad if he went round to see her for a while. Ivana was lying on the bed huddled under the eiderdown, shivering. There were dark circles under her eyes and her hair was hanging limply around her neck. She was reading through the letters Amos Elia had sent her. There were only a few of them she said, and they were rather short. He never wrote long letters. He did not have the patience. He had written those few short letters to her during the first few years they had known each other, when he thought she was important to him. Then he had stopped thinking she was important to him. He had got bored with her. Matteo Tramonti said that was not true. She said yes it was. It was true and there was no point in pretending otherwise. Carmine was holding both her hands, and stroking them. They were thin, pale, nervous hands. He had known them for a very long time. Isa Meli told her she was cruel to herself, and always had been. She loved to wound herself with every thought. Isa Meli was sitting by Ivana's bed knitting, Matteo Tramonti was playing chess with Angelica, while Daniele, Isa Meli's son, watched and made suggestions, because he was an excellent chess player, even though he was so young. The dog was asleep. Carmine thought how precocious Daniele was. Dodò knew nothing at all about chess, and his movements were so clumsy and unsure; he was not very alert either, he was behind for his age, thought Carmine. He was five years old, the same as Daniele. Perhaps they were giving him too much semolina. He was fat, and you do not give semolina to fat children. They should ask the paediatrician to put him on a different diet. He wondered what Daniele ate. He asked him what he had eaten for supper. Daniele said he had had cauliflower. 'With vinegar?' asked Carmine. Yes, of course, said Daniele. They never gave Dodò vinegar. He had never tasted a drop of vinegar in his life. He remembered the suppers of his own childhood. They were not even suppers really, just bits and pieces of leftovers on bread. 'Dodò always has semolina in the evenings,' he said. 'He drinks a lot of milk too; a litre a day.' 'Daniele can't drink milk,' said Isa Meli. 'It makes him sick.' 'He eats whatever comes to hand, pickles, salami, whatever he can find in the kitchen. But he's very strong, even though he looks so thin. Amos Elia used to say the thinner children are the better. He was a good doctor. He was particularly good at treating children. Whenever he came here, I always showed him the children straight away, and he examined them so thoroughly, from their hair right down to their toes. He used to have fun with them too. He was very patient. He always drew animals for them. He only came here a few times though.' 'He came here twice,' said Angelica. 'The first time he brought a salami, and the second time he brought some nuts. But the nuts were all black and empty inside.' 'Little vipew,' said Matteo Tramonti, 'all you can wemembew awe black empty things.' Carmine was very tired, and fell asleep in the armchair until, eventually, they woke him up and told him to go home because it was past midnight.

During the months that followed, Carmine was often reminded, in painful flashes, of the wizard's costume, and Ciaccia Oppi with her glasses perched on the end of her nose, absorbed in embroidering it with a big silver half-moon. At the fancy-dress party at Ciaccia Oppi's mother's villa in Velletri, Ninetta met a forty-year-old journalist, called Giose Quirino, and fell hopelessly in love with him. She already knew him a little, but having spent a long time with him in the kitchen making sandwiches and then hanging up paper chains in the hall, she fell in love. Carmine remembered too the moment they left for Velletri, Ninetta, Dodò and Ninetta's little sister Mariolina, in Ciaccia Oppi's car, with the wizard's costume and a Shirley Temple costume for Mariolina, consisting of a big blonde wig and a tiny, short, white organdy skirt with rosebuds. Ninetta was going to put on a black tunic and go as the Queen of the Night. During the afternoon, Ninetta phoned him and said she did not know whether to put on that black tunic, or whether to just wear old woollies and rags. She did not know whether to be the Queen of the Night, or a beggar. She could not make up her mind. Carmine thought at great length about that phone call later, because it was the last time they talked quietly and intimately. He said he was sorry he had not come, he did not like fancy-dress parties very much, and Queen of the Night or beggar, they were both nice ideas. Shuffling about in beggar's rags could be cute. He said he was sorry they had not been very affectionate towards one another of late, and that they had quarrelled a bit. He said perhaps they ought to take a little trip together somewhere, before long, to Perugia or Assisi. He had a burning desire to see paintings and churches and woods and fields, and stay in small hotels, even if they were a bit cold and uncomfortable, and get up early in the morning and plunge his feet into the dewy grass. She said perhaps they could go a little further afield, to Vienna or Prague, and that she wanted to see churches and paintings too, but she did not share his pressing desire for wet grass, partly because the villa in Velletri was rather damp. He said they would do whatever she preferred. She told him not to stay at home on his own, and to go downstairs and have dinner with her mother, or go to Ivana's, whichever he preferred, because their own cook was rather rude, especially when she had her period, and she seemed to remember that she had her period about now. If he decided to go to Ivana's, he could take the roast meat that was in the fridge, but not if he decided to go downstairs, because they were rather fussy about roasts downstairs. Then she said she had better go because of Ciaccia Oppi's phone bill.

The following day he went to fetch them. He knew the villa, and he knew Ciaccia Oppi's mother too, but had never realized before how gloomy they both were. It was morning. He entered a huge colonnaded room opening on to a vast, wet, leafy garden, and his longing for wet grass evaporated immediately. Ciaccia Oppi's mother was walking slowly up and down the room leaning on a silver-handled walking stick, while a nurse followed behind. She was inspecting the mess after the party, pointing with her stick to the scattered sweets, the remains of a broken glass in the fireplace and the stains on the carpet. She was the exact opposite of Evelina to look at, a tiny little old lady with a long face the colour of ivory and a hunched back, covered with a lace shawl. Carmine thought to himself how intolerable old people could be, even if they were the exact opposite of Evelina. Ciaccia Oppi, dressed in a housecoat and slippers, was scrubbing a sofa where someone had spilt a cup of hot chocolate. She was splashing soapy water on to the back of it from a small bottle. Ninetta, also in a housecoat, was helping her, rubbing energetically with a sponge. Her face was puffy and her eyes were swollen as if she had slept too long or had been crying, and she said she had a terrible headache because it had been a long, tiring party, starting with the children's tea-party in the afternoon. The adult party had carried on late into the night, but a few of the children had stayed up and so there had been constant noise. Dodò and Mariolina were still asleep. She went upstairs to wake them and get ready to go home. There was a general feeling of ill-humour all over the villa. Ciaccia Oppi and her mother were talking in peevish whispers; the nurse was looking mortified because the old lady kept telling her to stop following her around and that she was perfectly capable of walking by herself; the housekeeper, who had come to collect the dirty dishes, said it was no use wasting so much energy with those soap suds because the sofa was ruined. Dodò and Mariolina were bundled into the car, still half asleep, along with the bag of costumes and the toys they had been given at the party, and Ninetta got in beside Carmine, having kissed Ciaccia Oppi, who caressed her cheek with a sort of maternal commiseration, as if consoling her for a bereavement. The children slept off and on all the way home, and Ninetta looked out of the window and smoked, huddled into her raincoat. She answered Carmine's questions ill-temperedly. Yes, Dodò had looked beautiful, so had the silver half-moon, Shirley Temple too, of course. Her? no, not a beggar, the Queen of the Night. Carmine said he wanted a cappuccino. They had not even offered him a whiff of a cappuccino at the villa. What a mean old hag that woman was. It came out that Dodò might have been the one who spilt the chocolate on the sofa. But he said another boy had given him a push. It was a genuine Louis XV sofa, said Ninetta. Carmine went into the bar by himself, and Ninetta waited in the car with the children, her face still pale and puffy. As soon as they got home, she went and lay down on the bed, and, in the evening, when Carmine asked her if she wanted him to go to a travel agent's the next day, which was a Monday, and sort out that little trip to Vienna or Prague they had talked about over the phone, she replied later perhaps, in the spring or summer. Looking back on the days that followed, he could never make out just exactly at what point it became clear to him that, when she went out, she was not going to Ciaccia Oppi's, or to the supermarket, or to play tennis. But it was plain to see she was not going to any of those places. Carmine often found when he got in that Ciaccia Oppi was there for dinner, minus her husband, and after dinner, Ciaccia and Ninetta shut themselves in the little yellow room which had once been a playroom when Dodò was a baby. The play-pen was still there, and there were painted elephants and giraffes on the cupboards. Ninetta wanted everything left exactly as it was, because they might have a second baby. Dodò had a big playroom now, with a school desk, a globe and an abacus, ready for when he started school. Every so often, Carmine would knock on the door of the little yellow room, where Ciaccia and Ninetta were hiding, and ask whether Dodò was to have a bath or not, or whether the cook should order some ham. First Ninetta's plaintive murmur and then Ciaccia Oppi's shrill voice would answer yes or no. He had questioned Ninetta and now knew that she was having an affair with Giose Quirino and suffering badly, because she had always thought adultery was a sad, degrading thing. But although she was suffering, she was perhaps proud and stunned to be experiencing such a sad, degrading adventure. Her old radiant smile had gone, and in its place was a humble, tremulous, pained little smile. Carmine had met Giose Quirino at Ciaccia Oppi's house a few months before. He thought him the most ghastly imbecile. He was a tall, thin man with a face that was all furrows, wrinkles and bags, a grizzled forelock and pale eyes. His lean figure was always clothed in soft, elegant white sweaters. The first time she had seen him, Ninetta had said he looked like a monkey. There was that rag monkey of Dodò's, which was completely pulled to pieces now, its head was all floppy, but he always wanted to take it to bed with him. It could never be found in the evenings, and they always had to search the whole house for it. Ninetta had fished it out from under a piece of furniture one day, and said it looked like Giose Quirino. How long ago that moment seemed. Carmine had said Giose Quirino's bronzed, wrinkled, baggy face could be mistaken by the unwary for a rough, strong, weather-beaten face, and no doubt he was totally obsessed with whether the grimace that constantly contorted his lips was sufficiently wry and masculine. He was ghastly, said Carmine, a total imbecile. Ninetta had agreed. How long ago those tranquil moments and nods of agreement seemed. Carmine had said he looked as if he had just got back from Everest with that winter suntan, and Ninetta had said he got that tan at home with a sun-ray lamp. Ciaccia Oppi had told her so; he never went to the mountains, he had never set foot there in his life. He had a short, plump wife with a Piedmontese accent, who looked like a caretaker's wife. He also had a sixteen-year-old daughter, who was ugly and bespectacled. He did not like to take his wife and daughter around with him, but, sometimes, they refused to stay at home and attached themselves to him. His wife would go around telling everybody in her Piedmontese accent all the things he did not want people to know; about the exercises he did and the diets he followed in order to stay slim and trim, and the fact that he ordered his white jumpers cheaply, from a little shop he knew tucked away somewhere, which he never told anyone else about. The wry grimace grew softer and wearier when his wife and daughter were with him. Carmine found it strange and sad now, to think of Ninetta's delicate, fresh, white face next to that baggy, wrinkled one that was constantly twisted into an affected grimace. One day, Ciaccia Oppi came to his office in via della Vite. She had a big beaver hat on. It was March, but it was very windy, with gusts of rain and the odd flurry of sleet. Ciaccia Oppi told him Ninetta was hopelessly in love and planned to leave him, together with Dodò, and go and live with Giose Quirino. It was quite understandable too, she said. Carmine had neglected his home life for a long time; he spent hours and hours in via del Vantaggio. He could not be surprised at anything now. He said he was not surprised at anything, but he was not going to hand Dodò over to that ghastly imbecile. Ciaccia Oppi said, but that ghastly imbecile had shown himself capable of attentiveness, tenderness and dedication, qualities that Carmine might have once had, but had clearly forgotten. Carmine said he did not feel obliged to defend himself from her insinuations, that would be humiliating, but he was not depriving anyone of anything by spending a lot of time with Ivana; they had so many memories in common. Ivana and Angelica were the only trusted friends he had in the world. He immediately found it strange that he had named Angelica. He saw a mental picture of her tuft of hair and her one stern eye. Ciaccia Oppi's broad round face wore a sarcastic little smile, and he felt as if that smile and that hat had taken root in front of him and were indestructible. She went away at last, however, and he watched the beaver hat as it disappeared along the glass-covered corridor, swinging sarcastically from side to side.

A letter came from his parents. They said they would be

coming for Easter, as usual. His mother had knitted them a big red woollen cover for the double bed. She had remembered that they both liked red so much. He wrote and told them not to come. He said some cousins of Ninetta's were staying with them. These visits of his parents had grown increasingly tiresome over the years, because increasingly it seemed to him that although Ninetta and Evelina treated them with such gaiety and geniality, underneath it all they were heaving great sighs of boredom and hoping they would go away as soon as possible. Carmine was willing to bet that was how Evelina had always treated the nursemaid's family when Ninetta was a baby, giving them those big resounding kisses and stroking their shoulders protectively. When he and Ninetta had decided to get married, Evelina had found it difficult to accept the fact that Ninetta's parents-in-law would be two elderly peasants. But, in the end, she had managed to dress this strange, difficult idea in a rosy light because she always tended to dress everything that concerned her and everything that happened to her in a rosy light. She had been absolutely astonished to learn that Carmine's mother, whom she half carried around the house as if she were decrepit, was, in fact, five years younger than her. Furthermore, she was as solid as an oak, and quite accustomed, when she was at home, to washing her clothes in the stream and carrying sacks of wood. They had a washing-machine and a kerosene stove, but treated them both with suspicion. Evelina had suggested that Carmine should take his mother to their dentist, since she had such black, rotten teeth, but she had withdrawn the offer smartly, remembering that it took months to make a set of false teeth and besides, their dentist charged the earth for them.

When Carmine's parents got the letter telling them not to come, they were most offended and wrote back saying they would not have minded where they slept, a camp-bed would have done. However, they would not come if they were not welcome. They would send the cover by post. The cover came. It was orange really, not red at all, with a sort of green and black diamondy star in the middle. Ninetta thought it was horrible and threw it into the back of a cupboard. Carmine told her she must write and thank them though. She replied that she would. However, she never wrote letters, so in the end Evelina wrote for her, praising the wool and the star in the highest of terms.

Carmine knew that, although Evelina dressed everything that came into her life in a rosy light, she was completely unable to do so where Giose Quirino was concerned. She detested him with all her might. She thought he was hideous and indeed very much like a monkey. In the evenings, when she gave Dodò his rag monkey, she always raised her eyebrows and curled her lip and shook the floppy limbs contemptuously. Evelina detested all ugly people and loved beautiful ones, and she thought Carmine was very handsome. Besides, he was her son-in-law, and so, right from the start, although with some difficulty and doubt at first, she had endowed him with a solid uniform of shining light. It would take, at the very least, a lot of time to strip him of that uniform, and for the time being, she had brushed aside all the things about him she did not like, which were quite a few, and had lined herself up on his side. Giose Quirino, as she never tired of telling Ninetta in the mornings, while she was getting dressed or combing her fringe, or lacing her boots, was hideous, and quite apart from that, he was crude, ignorant and vulgar and his wife and daughter were both horrendous, and she thought the newspaper he wrote for was a terrible newspaper. She said he was politically very disreputable, because he had changed parties so many times and had now joined the Republican Party for opportunistic reasons. They had probably offered him a better job with another newspaper. He was morally disreputable too, because he was in the habit of getting drunk every evening. Ninetta refused to agree or disagree. She still wore that humble, tremulous fleeting smile on her face, but there was a sort of pride, too, in the way she shook her head and tossed her hair back behind her ears when she had done up the top button of her sandy-coloured camel jacket.

One day, Armandino phoned Carmine from Viterbo. Carmine was in bed at the time, with a bit of a temperature. It seemed to him as if the whole household had fallen apart. The cook was in the ironing-room talking to herself and saying that she wanted to leave because there was too much work to do, the light by the bed was not working, Dodò was wandering about on his own in a dirty jumper, and he had asked for some tea and it was not forthcoming. Ninetta was out and he had the phone beside the bed. He answered it listlessly, and, for a few moments, was unable to recognize this Armandino, whose warm, confidential voice was invading the misty void in which he lay suspended. Then he remembered. Ornella came to the phone too, and they fought over the receiver, vying with one another to tell him they were always thinking of him. All he had to offer was his feeble voice, hoarse with fever. They had found Amos's wife, said Armandino. She was not living in Berlin any more, but in Lübeck. She had a little shop that sold beauty products. She was not poor and did not seem anxious that they should sell the house. She had invited them to go to Lübeck. Perhaps they would some day. In the meantime, however, they wanted to come to Rome for a little trip very soon and see Carmine and Matteo Tramonti and dear Signora Riviera. They asked after the dog. He said it was very well. Really, he had not been to via del Vantaggio for about ten days, because the last time he had gone there, Ivana had been busy finishing a translation, so she was tired and edgy, and had screamed at him as soon as he had walked in the door that she could not care less about Ninetta and her love-life and the man with a face like a monkey, and she did not want to hear about it. He had said, but he needed to talk to someone about himself. What else were friends for? She had replied, but he never really came to her to talk about himself. If only he would talk about himself, but he always talked about daft, gloomy things instead. All he could do was worry his head about the man with a face like a monkey, and he knew very well that the man with a face like a monkey was completely beside the point, and his relationship with his wife had been on the rocks for a long time. He had put on his raincoat and left. He had not even phoned her. He felt angry and humiliated. He had looked for Matteo Tramonti, without success. Consequently, he did not know that the dog had fallen ill and died. He found out that afternoon. Ivana sent him a letter apologizing and asking him to come round and see her. The dog was dead. The vet said it had died of old age. But she thought it had died because it had been moved from the village. It must have been horrible for it to be in those three rooms and have to sleep in their kitchen and go out on that narrow balcony in the mornings. She understood how it felt. She found those rooms horrible too and would rather be somewhere else, but she was not sure where. If she did know where she would rather be, life would be better and everything would seem much more bearable. Although Angelica had always hated dogs, she had grown very fond of this one, and now she was wandering around the house like a lost soul and wanted another one.

In the course of that long afternoon, while his temperature was climbing, he found himself thinking that the best part of his existence was Ivana and all that surrounded her. No other source gave him that vital something which made him more intelligent, less ordinary and stronger. He had thought this many times before, but he thought it even more on this occasion. When Ninetta came in with her humble smile, her fringe somewhat ruffled, and her camel coat wet through from the rain, he felt sorry for her. She had a basketful of oranges in her hand. He had said he wanted some orange juice. But he had said it at three o'clock in the afternoon, and it was night-time now. She must have been troubled by the thought of the oranges while she was in the company of old wry face. He did not know where Ninetta and old wry face met, but he had an idea it was in an attic room above Ciaccia Oppi's flat in via Porpora, a room where she had put some of her old furniture and which had a separate entrance. Ninetta wanted to run and squeeze the oranges straight away, but he said he did not want orange juice now. He thought to himself that their relationship had been on the rocks for a long time. He could not say since when, since right from the beginning perhaps, but anyhow, he did not love her any more, although he did find her terribly pitiful. She sat down on the bed and told him the cook had given in her notice, and had told her as soon as she saw her walk in the door that she had come to them on the understanding she was to do cooking only, whereas, in reality, there was a whole heap of other work to do, and hardly any cooking at all. He said perhaps they should look for another one, depending on what their plans were for the future. But he did not want to talk or think about anything right now, because he had a terrible headache and a temperature, and he turned over to face the wall.

Next day, the doctor came and said it was pneumonia, so Ninetta spread a white cloth over the bedside-table and put the medicines on it, covered the lamp with a red headscarf of hers and unplugged the telephone and took it into the living-room. She did not dare go out any more, and moped about the house with a long face and disappeared into the living-room every so often to make a phone call. He told her she should go out. He did not need anything. Once, she did go out, leaving him with Evelina. Evelina loved looking after sick people, and she was there for the entire afternoon, sitting erect in the armchair with a dainty handkerchief in her hand, patting the cloud of blue hair around her forehead, smiling as one smiles at sick people and talking as one talks to sick people, with a few quiet, concise, light-hearted, calm words. Ivana and Matteo Tramonti came to see him several times, but he was an invalid, so they were not allowed into the room, and said hello to him from the doorway. Matteo Tramonti had never been to his house before, and on one occasion, he cast a quick glance around the living-room, saw the light over the table and whispered, 'It weally does look like a contwaceptive.'

At last, he was better and on his feet again. Ninetta said she wanted to see Ivana and talk to her. She had not had a chance to talk to her when she had visited him during his illness. So he called Ivana on the phone and asked her to come round straight away, by herself, not with Matteo Tramonti. Ivana came, and Ninetta took her into the yellow room. But she did not really know what to say to her. Perhaps she just wanted Ivana to see her in her present state of grand passion and torment and adulterous love. She said a lot of confused, complicated things, and stuttered, and groped for words and waved her hands around, without ever actually naming anyone. She wandered into abstractions. However, abstractions were not her strong point. In the meantime, Ivana stared at the brightly painted elephants and giraffes on the cupboards, and suddenly threw Ninetta completely by asking her why the play-pen was still there when they did not have any small children. Ninetta said they sometimes put her cousin's baby in there. Then Carmine came into the room in his pyjamas and brought them tea. He had made it himself, because although the cook was still there, she was too angry, on the whole, to make tea.

Then everything finished between Ninetta and Giose Quirino, and Ninetta just came in one evening, lay down on the bed and told Carmine in a flat voice that it was all over. Giose Quirino had said he did not want to see her any more, because he loved her too much, and it was hurting his wife too much. His wife was a diabetic and had a weak heart. He was bound to his wife and daughter by such a deep affection that their unhappiness made him tremendously unhappy too. Ninetta was able to get more than her fill of old wry face during those last few days of their relationship. They prolonged their good-byes for several days and dissected at length the nature and complexity of their union. Then Giose Quirino left for Corsica, because he had to do an article for his newspaper, and took his wife and daughter with him. Carmine had a suspicion that Evelina might have intervened through Ciaccia Oppi and offered Giose Quirino money to tell Ninetta they must end their relationship. But it was only a vague suspicion and might be an unjust one. Perhaps it really was his wife's diabetes that had led Giose Quirino to detach himself from Ninetta and from all those laborious secret rendezvous, and perhaps, deep down, he preferred his wife's quiet, domestic, undemanding bun to Ninetta's black fringe. Ninetta spent her days lying on the bed, looking pale, and staring vacantly into space watching her adultery fade into nothing. She asked to see Ivana again. Ivana came, and this time, they stayed in the bedroom. Ninetta just cried and Ivana tried to console her. However, as she said to Carmine afterwards, she was not made for consoling people. She found Ninetta profoundly stupid and absolutely pathetic. She could put up with her when she cried, but not when she wandered off into abstractions. She just did not know what course to advise her to take, she did not see any possible course. Evelina said to Carmine that it was time for him to rebuild their marriage. He tried to come home early from the office, and sat by the bed, silently stroking Ninetta's hand. They would call Dodò, and he would appear with his round, frightened eyes. Since the cook was no longer there, Evelina sent their dinners up to them and they ate in the kitchen. Summer came. Evelina had taken a big house in Poveromo, situated in a pine grove. This time, Carmine packed the bags, because Ninetta, who had always loved packing, just sat and stared at the empty suitcases, with tears rolling slowly down her nose. Carmine was afraid she might go mad. For the first few days at Poveromo, she lay on the veranda the whole time, like an invalid, and did not want to see anyone. Halfway through the summer, Evelina went away so that they could be alone to rebuild their marriage. Slowly, Ninetta became cheerful again, and returned to the things she liked doing, such as tennis, sailing, swimming and water-skiing, and she began to amuse herself by playing silly games in the pine grove with her friends; just a little at first, and then more and more. She developed an enormous craving for people, but had grown lazy and indifferent to what people might think of her. She insisted that people stay for supper, but could not be bothered to cook, so Evelina's servant had to do it. He did not know how to cook and ran back and forth looking flushed and terrified. The suppers were disorganized and bad. Ninetta had regained her old, broad, fixed, radiant smile which she offered like a jewel, and the flutter of the eyelids, and her limbs had recovered their long, graceful, languid movements. Her voice had recovered that childish, sing-song quality, which, no doubt, she secretly worshipped in herself, and which had disappeared at the time of her adulterous affair. Carmine breathed a sigh of relief because she had not gone mad. At one point, she told him she found it terribly humiliating to think that a short, fat woman with a prominent chest, scrawny legs like a chicken, and a faded bun, who spoke with a Piedmontese accent and looked like a caretaker's wife, had been chosen in preference to her. She could not care less about that man any more, she said. She hardly ever thought about him, but she did think about the short, fat woman, and it was very painful to her, almost as if someone were plunging red-hot irons into her vitals. However, that was the last time she ever spoke to Carmine about herself. He sometimes heard her talk about herself to other people, but it did not seem to him that she was being truthful. Now that he was no longer afraid she would go mad, he realized he was excruciatingly bored, but he stayed there in the house in the pine grove and took part in all those silly games with Ciaccia Oppi and friends of Ciaccia Oppi and friends of Ninetta, people to whom he had nothing to say. He returned to Rome at the end of August. Ninetta and Dodò stayed on at the seaside. Evelina, who had come back from Chianciano, stayed with them.

The house was dark when he arrived there early in the afternoon. The furniture in the living-room was covered with dust-sheets and the carpets were rolled up in a pile under the table. He looked again at the silkworm and the contraceptive and the globe and the abacus in the playroom next door. They had to enroll Dodò for school, and Ninetta had decided months ago, before her affair, that he would go to a beautiful German school with vast grounds and a minibus to take him there and bring him home. Months ago, too, she had prepared his school uniform, a blue overall edged in black, a big basket for his lunch and a red plastic satchel with the face of Sandokan on it. She always did things sooner than was necessary when she found them amusing, and at the time, the idea of having a child at school had amused her. But then, she had forgotten to enroll him. She had phoned the school from Poveromo and they had told her there were no places left, so now Carmine had to try and find him another school. It would probably have to be one with no grounds, no minibus, no lunch facilities and no German. Carmine continued to wander around the house for quite some time that afternoon, then he had a shower, wrapped his towel around him and went out on to the terrace in the blistering heat. The caretaker's wife had watered the flowers, but she had forgotten to feed the two tortoises. They were both lying dead, covered in ants, one amongst the fragments of a flower-pot, the other near the water butts. He threw away the two corpses and sprinkled the floor of the terrace with insecticide powder. Then he phoned via del Vantaggio. Angelica answered. Yes, he could come round. Yes, they had been to a camp-site in Sardinia with Isa Meli. Yes, it was nice there. Quite nice anyway. But they had had to go to the hospital in Sassari. Isa Meli had been ill. Oh, really, what had she had? A heart attack. My God. How was she now? All right. Olga was there. Who's Olga? he asked. Just Olga. Is she at Isa Meli's this Olga? he asked. No, here. Isa Meli's away, she's still in hospital in Sassari. But who is Olga? Olga's just Olga, O.K.

Olga had a big, squashed-looking nose and a large mouth that was always half-open, white teeth with gaps between them and long chestnut hair hanging loose about her shoulders. She was wearing baggy trousers rolled up to the knees and a big checked shirt. She was the one who opened the door to him, and held out a lean, brown, masculine-looking hand and said: 'Olga'. She took the parcel of food he had bought, which contained a roast chicken, mozzarella and some peaches, and went to put it all in the kitchen. She walked with light steps, flicking back her hair as she went. It was clear she liked to show people how familiar the house was to her, how she knew where everything went and could find the glasses and the knives immediately, and was completely used to laying the table. Carmine had sat down in the living-room with Ivana and Matteo Tramonti and was hearing all about the camping holiday and when Isa Meli had been really ill and they had had to take her to Sassari in a car Matteo Tramonti had borrowed. Matteo Tramonti was not staying at the camp-site at the time, but just happened to be nearby because he had gone to Sardinia with a group of musicians who were giving concerts. They had met Olga at the camp-site and she had not left their side since. She had gone to Sassari too, and waited with them in a motel for Isa Meli to recover. But they had had to leave Isa Meli there, because she had to stay in hospital for some time, so her two daughters had stayed with her, and they had come back to Rome with Daniele. Isa Meli would be home shortly, and Ivana and Olga had cleaned her flat from top to bottom, hung the curtains at the windows and ironed her nightdress and laid it on the bed ready so she could go to bed as soon as she got home. Carmine was listening and looking about him, happy to be back in that room again, listening to the voices of the only friends he had in the world. This Olga, whom they seemed to have grown so attached to, annoyed him a bit, but the way she moved around the house flicking her long hair this way and that was not displeasing to him.

They all sat at table and ate the roast chicken, the mozzarella, and meat-balls in tomato sauce cooked by Matteo Tramonti. Angelica dropped some tomato sauce on her skirt, and Matteo Tramonti said that skirt was filthy already anyway, then he said: "A giwl who weaws diwty clothes is a weal disgwace.'

Olga was twenty-seven. She was the daughter of a rich and famous orchestra conductor. She sometimes stayed at her parents' house, and sometimes with a sister, or with a friend who lived in via Salaria. At other times she stayed with a statistics student. They had a stormy relationship that had been going on for years. Like Matteo Tramonti, she chose where she wanted to sleep every night. She had a fully furnished flat of her own in via dei Greci, but never went there because the place filled her with horror for some reason. She knew some young people who had no money and they were staying there. It was a complete mess now, with sleeping-bags all over the floor. She had kept a room for herself, though, and asked that no one should sleep in there. But she did not know if they had taken any notice of her. She had a two-year-old son, who was with her sister. She said she loved him madly, but did not want the bother of bringing him up. His father was the statistics student. She was a writer, and had had a volume of poems published at her own expense, by a publisher in Catanzaro. The volume was called *Tigers and Pathways*. The poems were autobiographical and contained references to the statistics student. She told Carmine all this while he was driving her home in the mini, or rather, to the place where she had decided to sleep that night. She had decided to sleep at her friend's house in via Salaria.

Carmine had an affair with Olga which lasted two months and then finished abruptly. For a while, he felt as if he was very happy, and thought back over all the times when he had been happy before, when he had woken up in the morning to the feel of happiness surging over him like a warm river, sending all his thoughts swimming for the rest of the day in its clear, inviting water; drinking it in until they were filled to saturation point. He was not sure, at the time, whether that river was really flowing over him or whether he was just riding on old happy memories. Thinking about the girl months later, it seemed really strange to him that he should have thought she could change his life in any way. They used to meet in her room in via dei Greci, going round by a long balcony to get in, so as not to have to climb over all the sleeping-bags. Then they walked, talking endlessly, through streets that seemed strange and new to him one moment, and welcoming and easy to walk along the next. In fact, they were the same streets he walked along every day, and normally he found them boring, hostile and inhospitable. Sometimes, they had dinner in via del Vantaggio, and it seemed so strange to watch her move about those rooms he had known for so many years. It made him happy. On other occasions, they collected Angelica from school, or went to the theatre in Flaminio to fetch Matteo Tramonti, or hear him sing and play. She always wore the same baggy trousers and checked shirt, but when it started to get cold, she tied a jumper round her shoulders, and afterwards, looking back on those days, he remembered that about the time of the jumper, their relationship had started to dissolve into nothing, into a frivolous superficial happening, a useless, forgettable detail.

He had thought about living in a proper house with her. But then that seemed like an absurd idea, and so did the endless conversations and his severity towards her. He *was* severe with her. He tried to get her to look after her son and give up her restless, ageing rich adolescent's ways. A cold little smile started to appear on her lips, and when he noticed he was getting this cold little smile more and more frequently in reply to his severity, he realized that it was falling on stony ground.

In mid-September, Ninetta had gone to Lake Maggiore with Ciaccia Oppi, leaving Dodò with Evelina in Poveromo. Consequently, Dodò missed quite a few days of school, but Ninetta had decided he should spend a long time at the seaside, because it was good for him and he enjoyed it so much. In the end, they had enrolled him at a convent school, which had no minibus, but it did have grounds and they served lunches there. The blue overall edged with black was not suitable for that school. The children there wore white overalls, and Evelina phoned from Poveromo, asking Carmine to buy a white overall from Upim, so that it would be ready for Dodò when he got home. Carmine went to Upim and bought the overall, and hung it in the playroom next to the globe and the abacus.

Ninetta came back by plane, from Milan, with Ciaccia Oppi. He went to the airport to collect them and found Ninetta looking slim and suntanned, wearing a new white overcoat. Shortly afterwards, that same morning, Evelina arrived, with her servant and Dodò. They had to find a cook, or what Ninetta insisted on calling a cook, despite the fact that she expected her to do everything and only excused her from cleaning the windows, because Evelina's servant came to do that. With the help of Ciaccia Oppi, a cook was found. Carmine was thinking to himself that, later, when Ninetta had rested and unpacked her bags, when the dust-sheets had been taken off the sofas, he would tell her he had had a girlfriend for some time, and that she was not entirely unimportant to him. However, he always tended to procrastinate, and the bags had been unpacked and the dust-sheets taken off the sofas for several days, and the cook had spring-cleaned and tidied the whole house, and he still had not told her. Now he was the one cultivating an illicit affair right under her nose, without her knowledge. He felt he was being much more cunning and hypocritical than she was, because there were probably no outward signs in his expression or bearing. While she was away, he had thought he would not feel in the least bit guilty, but when she got into bed beside him, in her green voile nightdress, or when she got dressed in the morning, or combed her black fringe, or looked at herself intently, putting her cheeks and chin and lips right up close to the mirror, he did feel a strong sense of guilt towards her, so strong and cold, in fact, that he could feel himself going pale. He would take Dodò to school and watch him walk away into the vast grounds of the convent school, on his fat little legs, with his white overall showing beneath his coat and the red satchel with the face of Sandokan on his shoulders. Then he would think about Olga's son, whom he had never seen. She did not want him to. She always used to say he could see him later, but not now. He imagined them all living together in a house, himself, Olga, the other little boy and Dodò.

Ninetta found out about Olga from Ciaccia Oppi. Ciaccia Oppi had a thousand ears, and nothing ever escaped her where love affairs were concerned. They were the only thing in the world that really interested her. She thought the world very boring, but thank goodness, there were love affairs, eternally beginning and ending, performing arabesques and pirouettes in the universal dullness. Besides, Carmine had made no secret of his relationship with Olga, for some time they had been walking around town together and eating together in restaurants. When Ninetta found out, she behaved in a quite unexpected way. She told Carmine nonchalantly that she knew he had a girlfriend and she couldn't care less. She was a girl who went around in dirty trousers, a dirty mac and tatty sandals and had long untidy hair. She also had a child she had foisted on to her sister because she could not be bothered with him. Carmine said it was all true except the mac. There was no mac. Ninetta said perhaps it would be better if they separated. But, on the other hand, no, perhaps it would be better if they waited until Dodò had got used to going to school. Carmine pointed out that Dodò was perfectly happy going to school. Yes, but you could never tell, said Ninetta. Carmine found her a completely changed person. Her voice had become dry and hard, and there were two slight furrows on her full, milky cheeks. She smiled very little, and only when there were people about. She had enrolled at an art school, and asked Ciaccia Oppi if she could rent her attic. She went there every morning to paint, and did abstract paintings, using big, fat dollops of colour. A painter, a friend of Ciaccia Oppi's, told her they were interesting. She built castles upon this word. She did not bother with the house, but just barked out a few cross words at the cook every morning before she left. They changed cooks two or three times in the space of a month. Then came an elderly cook, who was very mild, although rather dirty, and whom Ninetta treated reasonably kindly. Ninetta quarrelled furiously with Ciaccia Oppi over a damp spot in the attic. Nevertheless, she kept the attic on, because she found it convenient. But she had a new circle of friends, and said she was fed up with Ciaccia Oppi. Evelina had not been told about Olga, and every time she saw Carmine she repeated that he must be very patient with Ninetta, and very cautious and steady because that was the only way they would rebuild their marriage.

Carmine's parents wrote and asked if they could come. It was not Easter, it was All Souls, but they wanted to come anyway, and Carmine's mother wanted to see a good doctor because she had a severe blood disorder. He could not put them off this time. They came. Carmine had to accompany them to the doctor's and stay in with them in the evenings, and he felt he wanted to strangle them. He loved them, but he could just have strangled them. Ninetta had taken the orange cover Carmine's mother had made out of the cupboard and put it on the bed. Evelina held forth on the softness of the wool, and on the star in the middle and the admirable contrast between the orange and the green. Carmine felt he wanted to strangle Evelina too, in fact he wanted to strangle Evelina above all. Then there were Dodò's exercise books to be admired, and his drawings and the globe and the abacus and the goldfish in the round bowl. Ninetta was always out and did not come home until dinner time. It soon became clear to Carmine's parents that Ninetta's behaviour towards them had changed. Gone were the big smacking kisses and the cheeses and fruit she had ferreted out from the other side of town. Gone was the smile. Evelina's smile was still there, but even that was a bit wearier and less attentive. They thought Ninetta might be ill. They suggested to Carmine that perhaps she was over exerting herself and needed to get more rest. The days passed, and they realized more and more that something had happened, something secret and tragic, something it was better not to talk about. At dinner time they sat bolt upright at the big glass table, underneath the dangling contraceptive, and fed small pieces of bread into their mouths in embarrassed silence. Carmine adored and detested their wrinkled faces, their long, straight, crepy necks, their black clothes and their knowing silence of old folks who have understood. They went home again, and it was an enormous weight off Carmine's shoulders to take them to the station and put them on the train. Yet at the same time, he felt the most heart-rending sadness.

Ninetta did not want to put the bedspread back in the cupboard. She left it on the bed. She said, after all, it was quite nice and warm, and it did not matter that it was so hideously ugly. 'You can get used to anything,' she said flatly, shrugging her shoulders.

As soon as Carmine had seen his parents off on the train,

he went to via dei Greci, where Olga was waiting for him. Lately, he had only seen her fleetingly for the odd half hour. He wanted to talk to her about his parents, and how much he had adored and detested them these last few days. But she was very distracted and he did not manage to tell her anything.

In the months that followed, Carmine could never make out just exactly when he had stopped imagining that he and Olga could live together. When the desire for happiness and the memory of happiness had finally left him, and at which moment of which day he had first realized it. Olga simply started to ring him at the office more and more often, to cancel their dates. She had to see the statistics student because he was depressed. She had to meet her sister and go to the lawyer's office with her to sign some papers. She had to go to the cinema with some young people she had met who were rather fun. He started to question her, but the only reply he got was a tight, cold little smile, then a rapid flick of her soft hair. Her gaze was elsewhere. In the end, she told him she had someone else, and she was tired of him. He wanted to know who it was. Just a boy, she said. For some time, she had felt an enormous desire to be with a boy, someone who took life lightly, even though he might be a bit melancholy. Carmine on the other hand, was so grown-up and stern and heavy. He led a heavy life, and forced her to carry that weight too. He judged her harshly because she did not keep her son with her. He disapproved. Well, she would not tolerate disapproval. She wanted to be accepted as she was. He said even if he did speak to her severely, that did not mean he regarded her with one jot less understanding. She said, yes, but she wanted to be accepted as she was a bit more. But it was not really about that. She just liked this boy, and she never had long-lasting relationships anyway. She might go away with the boy for a while, to the seaside or somewhere. He must stop thinking about her. It was over.

For Carmine, this marked the beginning of a period of intense work, because he had started writing the book on the suburbs of modern towns and cities, an idea he had had for some time. He either worked in his office in via della Vite, or at home, in the living-room, by the silkworm. The happiness he had felt throughout those months had been confused and unreal, perhaps he had just invoked it from the realms of obscure shadows and memories, perhaps he had called it that simply because he wanted to get up and wave a banner in the name of happiness. The unhappiness, however, was real, and had nothing whatsoever to do with shadows and memories. It dominated his existence as if it had always been there. It woke him early in the mornings, as if it were planting great forests and mountains over his outstretched body. He would get up and go into the kitchen to make a cup of coffee. Their mild-mannered old cook would be there, her grey plait hanging down her back, half undone. She would say something to him about the weather, or the radiators, or the plumber, or Dodò. He would reply in a low voice, with great effort. He talked very little now, and always in a low voice, because it was difficult for him to get his words out from underneath the forests and mountains of unhappiness. He told Ninetta one evening, in this low, feeble voice, that it was all over between him and the famous girlfriend she had heard so much about. Ninetta said nothing. Her only comment was that he spoke so softly these days, as if someone in the house had died. Carmine replied in the same low voice that he would try and talk louder, but his real wish was not to have to talk at all, to anyone. Slowly, with great effort, he tried to talk to Dodò, while he was driving him to school in the morning, or while he was sitting by the little red table in the playroom, in the evening, waiting for him to finish his semolina. Basically, he thought to himself, he must avoid all contaminated places. Contaminated places were those where he had thought, however waveringly and uncertainly, that that woman was something more than a trivial, forgettable event in his life. There were contaminated places all over town, now, but some places were especially unbearable. There was no way he could go into the restaurant below his office, the café below his office or Ivana's house. Then he told himself the whole thing was ridiculous, because even if he avoided those particular cafés and restaurants, he could not avoid the streets, and nearly every street in town was sick and infested, swarming with pestilent memories of wasted moments. Ivana told him he should go away for a while; take a trip somewhere. She was not usually patient and sympathetic where unhappiness was concerned. She used to say you should be ruthless with your unhappiness, tear it out and trample it underfoot. However, this time she was careful, and docile and gentle with him. He did not want to take a trip though. He did not want to budge an inch. He just wanted to cling to the book he had started writing. Ivana and Matteo Tramonti used to come and fetch him from his office and go with him, not to the restaurant down below, but to another one on the corner of the street, where he had not been very much in the past. Matteo Tramonti told him repeatedly 'that giwl was not wowth a liwa', he had known it all along, right from the first moment he had seen her. They had all fallen for it, Ivana, Angelica, Isa Meli, Isa Meli's daughters, even Daniele. They had treated her as if they would all be together forever. They had fallen for it like pears. Ivana said she was a terribly neurotic person, and all right, perhaps, at rock bottom. 'At wock bottom,' said Matteo Tramonti, 'we'we down to wock bottom awe we? We'we all all wight at wock bottom. Well, pewhaps not all of us, but neawly all. *Tigews and Pathways*,' he said, 'how could anyone publish a book with such a widiculous title. *Tigews and Pathways* indeed.' Olga had never shown herself again. She had phoned Ivana once about a jacket she had lent Angelica and which she wanted back. 'Thewe, you see,' said Matteo Tramonti, 'she's a misew too.' Angelica had taken the jacket back to where Olga's sister lived, and left it in the caretaker's office. As she was leaving, she had met Olga and her sister and the baby, at the front door. He was a lovely baby. Olga had just said 'Hi,' not even 'Hi, thanks,' and had strode off immediately, her sandals flapping as she went, her jumper tied round her waist. 'To think,' said Matteo Tramonti, 'that she spent all that time eating and dwinking in youw house, and you would have thought the house, the food and evewything wewe all hews.'

Ivana told Carmine that he must stop all this nonsense about contaminated places, however, and start going to all the places where he used to go. She said he must exorcise them all. She said when Amos Elia had died, she had had to exorcise various parts of the town where she had walked with him, or where they had met. Matteo Tramonti was right really, she said, that girl was not worth a great deal. Carmine had built her up in his mind out of an absolute need to build a woman for himself and place her in the centre of his existence. Carmine went back to his old habit of sitting in the armchair in via Vantaggio every evening, looking out over the roof-tops, the bridge, the winding river and the cars blocking the street below. He started going with Ivana and Angelica once again to the theatre in the Flaminio district where Matteo Tramonti and his friend Giulio Grimaglia sang and played nearly every night. It was always crowded with people. Sometimes, the fat lady lawyer was there, with her lame leg stretched out on a stool. There were wooden benches and wooden stairs. On the stage was some black tubular scaffolding that had been used for a comedy and never taken down.

Then Carmine stopped being so silent, and feeling tired every time he tried to speak. He stopped avoiding certain streets and certain places in town. For all that it had seemed impossible to him, at times, he stopped thinking about Olga, and when he did think about her, her face wove in and out of his thoughts, along with a thousand others. He started to think about Ninetta again, not lovingly, but with a sort of melancholy, petty curiosity. Little quarrels would break out between them every so often. They were acrimonious quarrels, but completely devoid of anger, their voices remained calm. Listening to them from another room, no one would have thought they were arguing. These quarrels were caused by small things, the plumber, the radiators, the cook, and they evaporated as quickly as they had started. Carmine forgot them immediately, they just left him with a general feeling of unease which he could not quite place, and which stayed with him for the rest of the day. They spent long hours together, when there was great calm. She would be on the sofa with her fringe all ruffled, reading a book. He would be sitting nearby, absorbed in sketching something carefully on to a sheet of paper, with a fine brush and Indian ink, while Dodò watched him. There would be cars, motor bikes, traffic-lights and people scattered about everywhere because Dodò had to draw a picture for school entitled 'my district'. But these periods of calm did not produce any real feelings of peace, just as the quarrels did not produce any real feelings of anger. The mild-mannered old cook left, and a new one came. According to Ninetta, this one was even dirtier. They quarrelled regularly. Dodò's school put on a play, and Carmine, Ninetta and Evelina went to see it. Evelina wore an enormous black hat. They spent two hours watching Dodò standing quite still in one corner of the stage dressed as an officer of Napoleon, wearing a red cloak and carrying an enormous drum. Ninetta said to Carmine that since they never came in at the same time in the evenings, and one of them always woke the other up, it would be better if he moved to the room next door to the playroom. This was a long narrow room that had never been used much. It was intended to be a dining-room for when they had a lot of guests, because it was equipped with a large cupboard which Ninetta did not like. She had a box mattress and a wardrobe put in there, and said she would soon find another place for the cupboard so that the room would look like a bedroom. However, the cupboard stayed where it was because a suitable place could not be found, and besides, Carmine did not find it particularly strange that the room where he slept should have a huge, inlaid ebony sideboard full of china and glassware that tinkled every time a bus went by.

It was all temporary anyway, and they were both thinking they would separate sooner or later. When the hot weather came, Evelina asked Ninetta where she was thinking of going for her holidays, but at the mention of the word 'holidays', Ninetta became very vague, and it was soon quite clear that she did not want to know about renting villas, unless her mother would like to rent one and take Dodò there. But Evelina was without her servant, he had left to take a job in a warehouse. She just had a charlady now, and cooked for herself in the evenings. She had sent her younger daughter, Mariolina, to study in England, so she did not want to know about renting villas either, and said really, the best place to stay was in a hotel, but she could not leave Rome because she had workmen in her house, so her holiday would be going to Fregene every morning with a hired chauffeur, while her charlady kept an eye on the workmen.

'This is a pain,' said Angelica. 'What's a pain?' asked Carmine. 'Staying here.' They were still sitting in the café, even though Dodò had quite finished eating his gypsy sundae and was gazing in wonder at the people sitting all around, and Daniele was wandering in and out of the tables from sheer boredom and evening was coming on. 'It's a pain staying here,' said Angelica. 'Why, where would you rather be?' asked Carmine. 'I don't know, but not here.' 'That happens to me too, all the time,' said Carmine. 'I'm not happy where I am, but I haven't the faintest idea where I would rather be, nor, most important of all, who I would rather be with.' 'I really don't want to go home,' said Ivana. 'I'd like to have supper with you,' said Carmine. 'At the restaurant I hope,' said Angelica, 'there's nothing to eat at home.' 'I've invited Signora Tattoli to supper,' said Ivana, 'so I've got to go home. It won't be long before she arrives.' 'Who's Signora Tattoli?' asked Carmine. 'The woman who lives on the floor above. She's the landlady.' 'Why have you invited her to supper?' said Angelica, 'We haven't even got anything to eat.' 'There's the rice salad,' said Ivana. 'That's not much,' said Angelica, 'and anyway, it's yesterday's, and it looks like yesterday's, you can always tell when something's left over.' 'We could come too,' said Carmine. 'I don't know about that. Our landlady's not much fun,' said Ivana. 'I don't care about having fun,' said Carmine. 'I can buy a roast chicken and come on later. You can just give Dodò an egg to drink.' 'He's the one who eats semolina. Isn't he?' said Angelica. 'No, not any more,' said Dodò. 'I used to eat semolina all the time, now I like spaghetti with butter.' 'We haven't got any spaghetti,' said Angelica. 'What's this then? This looks like spaghetti,' said Carmine. He pushed back the long strands of hair from her forehead, and the hidden eye appeared for a split second. 'But why invite your landlady?' said Carmine. 'I met her on the stairs this morning, while I was with Isa Meli. She was admiring Isa Meli's jumper and said she would like to learn how to do the stitch.' 'But Isa Meli knows how to do the stitch, not you, so it would have been better if Isa Meli had invited her to supper,' said Angelica. 'I've invited Isa too. The truth is, we want to ask her to prolong our tenancy agreement. We're both afraid of the rent act. If it goes through, she could put our rent up a lot or throw us out.' 'You won't save yourself from the rent act with rice salad,' said Carmine. 'But, on second thought, we won't come, there would be too many of us with the landlady and Isa Meli.' 'There's Olga!' said Angelica, 'Down there, sitting on the steps of the monument eating a banana. She's got a dog with her. It's huge, it looks like a bear.' 'Bears and pathways,' said Carmine. 'It's strange, but I don't care about her any more.' Olga got up. She passed close to their table. She said 'Hi' and moved on, pulling the dog behind her. 'Is that all she's got to say, hi?' said Angelica. 'She was always at our house. She used to come round early in the morning and ring the bell really hard as if she had something important to tell us, or something important to do there, but she never did anything. She never said anything much. She tried our clothes up against herself, and washed her hair and got herself bread and jam for breakfast, then she sat down on the carpet and played patience, and that was all. But she was always there, and now she hardly says hello.' 'She's a girl who's always looking for places to go,' said Ivana. 'Above all, she's looking for mothers, fathers and brothers. Then she gets bored. The ones she's found seem wrong for her. She feels she's landed up in the wrong place, so she looks for another.' 'I think she must have seen a father in me,' said Carmine, 'but I was too strict for her.' 'Or too weak,' said Ivana. 'I don't know,' said Carmine. 'I don't really care now, not one bit.' 'You once said that, a long time ago, when you and my mother lived together, you quarrelled a lot,' said Angelica, 'and now you don't quarrel at all, you chat to each other and you get along quite well. And you're always at our house, like Olga used to be. You don't ring the bell early in the morning, but you're always there. When you were together, when you had that baby daughter who died, you used to quarrel, but now you don't any more. Perhaps you should have stayed together, then in the end you would have stopped quarrelling and got used to chatting peacefully together.' 'I don't think so,' said Ivana. 'I don't think so either,' said Carmine. 'But we didn't leave each other because of the quarrels,' said Ivana. 'Well, why then?' asked Angelica. 'I don't know any more,' said Ivana. 'It was such a long time ago.'

Carmine had changed his mind and decided to have supper with them even if Signora Tattoli was going to be there. He bought a roast chicken, mozzarella and some wine, and they all went upstairs. Carmine sat in the armchair while Angelica set the table and Isa Meli chopped up some runner beans, which were also left over for that matter, but she thought the rice salad was a pathetic-looking offering quite apart from being left over. Angelica told him it was disgraceful that he was just sitting there doing nothing, but he said he was tired and did not feel too well, he felt as if he had a clamp round his head. Dodò had fallen asleep in one corner of the settee, and they had got Daniele peeling some cold left-over boiled potatoes Isa Meli had brought. She said they could be fried up in butter. Signora Tattoli came. She was an elderly woman with dyed red hair. Matteo Tramonti came too, unexpectedly, and Signora Tattoli asked him to play. She loved the guitar, and had heard him play once in the theatre in Flaminio, but the seats there, she said, were hard, narrow and uncomfortable. Matteo Tramonti played and sang. Signora Tattoli left early, not long after supper, and Angelica pointed out that Isa Meli had taught her the knitting stitch, but no one had mentioned the rent agreement. In fact, Ivana had been waiting for Isa Meli to mention it and Isa Meli had been waiting for Ivana to mention it, and it was not until the very last moment, when Signora Tattoli already had her foot on the doormat, that Ivana expressed a desire to spend the rest of her days in the flat. Signora Tattoli just smiled. Carmine said he was very tired and he was going too. He was only sorry that he had to wake Dodò who was sleeping so peacefully in the next room, on Angelica's bed. He stayed a little while longer to look at them all, Ivana, Angelica sitting at the table with her tuft of hair dangling, and Matteo Tramonti sitting cross-legged on the carpet with his guitar and his fluffy beard.

When he and Dodò arrived at the front door of their house, he realized he did not feel like lifting the garage door open as he usually did every evening, so he gave up. He left the car parked in the street. They were greeted by the au pair girl, in baby-doll pyjamas, who took Dodò off to bed. Carmine went to bed in the room with the dresser.

He spent a fretful night, hating the dresser. It was clearly visible in the half light and became suddenly illuminated from time to time by the headlamps of passing cars because the blinds did not close properly. He hated the way the plates jumped about and clattered every time a bus went by, hated the words of the song Matteo Tramonti had sung that evening, which were now fluttering around like flags in his mind and battling with his sleep. 'Di sangue han sporcato i cortili e le porte / chissà quanto tempo ci vorrà per puliri.' [They have stained the courtyards and doorways with blood, Who knows how long it will take to clean them.] He could not move to the double bedroom, because, before Ninetta had left for Venice, she had called in some decorators to whitewash the walls, so the floor was still covered with newspapers and the bed had no mattress, and was covered in newspapers and dust-sheets. 'Compagni, dai campi a dalle officine / prendete la falce, prendete il martello,' the song went on. [Comrades from the fields,

Comrades from the factories, Take up the hammer, take up the sickle.] He had also heard Matteo Tramonti and his friend Giulio Grimaglia sing it at the theatre in the Flaminio district, where, as Signora Tattoli had rightly said, the seats were rather narrow and uncomfortable. The song was called 'Contessa', and told the story of a strike. Matteo Tramonti loved it. Carmine preferred other songs, but could not remember which ones they were that night. He was assailed by an acute nostalgia for the evenings he had spent in that theatre, those uncomfortable seats and dusty boards decked out with red curtains. It seemed to him that those evenings, and others he remembered spending with Matteo Tramonti and Ivana in the streets, cafés and piazzas, were part of a remote, lost era. All night, he struggled with snatches of song, flashes of light and the tinkling of glasses, and, by the end of it, he was exhausted and sweating. Morning came at last, and he opened the shutters and told the au pair girl whom he met in the corridor that he thought he had a fever. Evelina came, majestic, smiling and reassuring. They made him a cup of tea, re-made the bed for him and called the doctor.

After that, everything seemed simpler and a little better than the night had been, with its flashes of light, and the song 'Contessa' and the tinkling of glasses. He had a temperature. The doctor said he thought it was a virus infection. He was not sure yet exactly what it was. Carmine lay there quietly, feeling tired. They brought him mineral water and newspapers. The au pair girl came to say good-bye to him because she had to go to her Italian course. The caretaker's wife came. Evelina went to Fregene with Dodò, the same as she did every morning.

He phoned Ivana, but there was no one in, so then he phoned Isa Meli and she told him Ivana and Angelica had gone to spend a few days in the country, at Farfa, with Matteo Tramonti and his friend Giulio Grimaglia. Matteo Tramonti's mother had a house there. The house was perched high on a hill and had no telephone. They had decided to go there the evening before, just after he left. He felt very much alone.

He told Isa Meli he was ill, and she reminisced at length about her heart attack in Sardinia, when she had thought she was going to die. She offered to come and keep him company, but he thanked her and said there was no need. They talked for a while about Ivana, and about Signora Tattoli and the rent agreement, then about Matteo Tramonti's mother's house at Farfa, with its magnificent view of the whole valley.

In the evening he had a high temperature, so they moved him to the double bedroom, which had been put back in order, and was the same as ever except for a slight smell of fresh paint. For several days he was on his own, and Evelina, or the au pair girl or the caretaker's wife appeared from time to time. Then Ninetta came home, and the room filled up with her suitcases and clothes. 'Was it nice in Venice?' he asked, in a voice that was slightly hoarse with fever, and also because he had not talked for some time. Ninetta indicated with a movement of her chin that it was and carried on hanging up her clothes and removing little balls of tissue paper from the inside of her shoes. She was irritable, and seemed quite unprepared to come face to face with an illness. She took the telephone into the living-room, and was continually in and out making phone calls. The doctor said the same thing to Ninetta, that he did not know exactly what was wrong. They would have to take some tests, but it did not seem to be anything serious, there were no particular symptoms apart from the fever. He did not complain of any pain, just a clamp-like feeling around his head, and a slight difficulty in breathing. Suddenly, Ninetta was a bit frightened, a confused, lost look appeared in her eyes. Several more days passed, and everything was just as it had been when he had pneumonia, Ninetta's red scarf over the light, the white cloth over the bedside table and the medicines and hypodermic syringes, Ninetta's long, delicate body moving about the room, Evelina sitting erect by his bed, holding the same little handkerchief. Only this time, things seemed to be going a completely different way. The doctor said they had better take him into the clinic. Ninetta and Evelina took him there in the mini. In the clinic, the windows had yellow curtains with black lozenges on them, and after he had been lying there for a few minutes, Carmine realized that those black lozenges were all he had left to rest his eyes upon. He realized he had been ill for a week, because it was Sunday, and it was only a week since he had been to the cinema with Ivana and Angelica and the boys, and they had seen the film *Abyss*, with the millionaires and the sharks, and when they had come out of the cinema, they had sat in that café in the square, then there had been the supper, Signora Tattoli and the song 'Contessa'.

Ivana and Matteo Tramonti came. They had just got back from Farfa, where they had cooked, picked mushrooms, sunbathed and written a plot for a film, together with Giulio Grimaglia. They explained the plot to him. Carmine found it long, boring and badly put together, with far too much happening, so he stopped listening after a while. Ivana was wearing her usual blue T-shirt, faded almost white from repeated washing. Her hair was not twisted into a topknot, it was hanging loose, in a short, bristly pony-tail, and she played with it as she talked. Matteo Tramonti said they could make money with that plot. 'Don't you agwee, it's a mawvellous plot?' he said. Carmine smiled absently. Suddenly, he noticed Ivana had stopped talking and was looking at him anxiously, while Matteo Tramonti was still racking his brains over the story of drugs, diamonds, airports and blood. Seeing her look so anxious, Carmine felt he wanted to reassure her, and he started racking his brains, along with Matteo Tramonti, over the intricacies of the plot.

Next day, Ivana came on her own. She stayed with him all afternoon, and they were alone together, because Ivana had told Ninetta to go home and get some rest. She asked Carmine whether he had already been feeling ill the Sunday they had gone to the cinema to see *Abyss*, and, if so, why had he not told her. He said he had not felt particularly ill that day, he had just been tired and had a bit of a headache; he had told Angelica when she had got angry with him for not helping her to lay the table. Ivana said they had talked so quietly together that Sunday at the café. Carmine said that, now, thinking back on that Sunday, it seemed like a very nice day, and yet, he had not noticed it at the time, because there was nothing wonderful about going to see a bad film, nor about sitting in a café, ordering ice-creams and waiting for the evening to come. He felt an agonizing nostalgia for that day now, and yet, they had been bored sitting in that café, thinking they would spend thousands more days like that one, just as they had done in the past, because there was nothing so easy and mindless as sitting in a café for a few hours. After that, they said nothing for a while, and she played with her hair as it hung in that bristly pony-tail. All of a sudden, he said, 'Do you remember the baby?' He asked her if she ever went to the cemetery. She said, 'No, I hate cemeteries,' and he laughed and said, 'I hate them too.' She said she did not feel there was any connection between the cemetery and their baby, nor between the cemetery and Amos Elia, and she felt the dead stayed well away from cemeteries. Perhaps they hated them too, and went in search of other places, different ones every day. It had never entered her head to go to the cemetery in Fontechiusa, where Amos Elia was buried, but she did sometimes feel she wanted to go and see Ornella and Armandino's electrical shop in Viterbo. She could not bear those two, but there were times when she wanted to pay them a visit for some unknown reason. Other times, she thought about going to Lübeck, where Amos Elia's wife had her cosmetics shop, to see if she was really as she had always imagined her to be, or whether she was completely different. Then Carmine said that, as a child, he had gone to the cemetery every Sunday, with his mother, and the only cemetery he had never hated was the one in his village, which was in the open countryside, on a dip in the road.

He still wanted to talk about the baby. 'It did not seem so amazing to me then, to have a baby,' he said, 'but it was all you could think about at the time, and you took her out on your parents' terrace every day. It took you half an hour to get there on the bus, and we had a nice sunny terrace of our own. I thought you were mad.' 'It was a bit too sunny, that terrace of ours,' she said, 'there wasn't a patch of shade and not a tree in sight; nothing but roofs. There was no chlorophyll. Besides, when I went to my parents' they kept an eye on the baby, and it gave me a breather.' 'Yes, I remember you were always talking about chlorophyll,' said Carmine, and he laughed. 'But I was jealous of your parents, and I didn't like them. And yet, when your father came to collect your suitcases, just after the baby died, I suddenly liked him very much, he was so kindly looking and so sad.' 'My parents criticized the way we lived, and ate and spent our money,' said Ivana, 'nothing was right for them. But it's the same now that I'm living on my own. I still can't do a thing right.' 'I often think about the times we were together,' said Carmine, 'and I remember so many things now, that I'd forgotten. I remember the green tiles in the shower-room, and the stand in the hall, the one that I made, which fell over every time we put our coats on it because it couldn't take the weight.' 'I'd forgotten that hall stand,' said Ivana, 'I wiped everything about the flat from my memory after the baby died, it was all too painful to me.' 'But I've never felt we were wrong to leave one another,' said Carmine. 'No, I've never thought so either,' said Ivana.

Carmine lived for another two months. At times, the idea of dying seemed horrible to him, and he tore it from his mind because he could not bear it. At other times, he was borne aloft by his thoughts, and flew, light fleeting and cold, like a snowflake. He was not told the name of his illness, which was malignant lymphogranuloma, but he overheard Evelina and one of the doctors talking about it in a corridor, while they were wheeling him out of the X-ray room. His parents came. He saw them there in their black clothes, perched on the little sofa at the far end of the room. They were sitting upright as usual and their wrinkled faces wore a tight-lipped expression. They were staring fixedly down at their hands which were clasped between their knees. Sometimes he asked to see Dodò, and they brought Dodò to him dressed in his light autumn overcoat made of Scotch wool. He looked frightened, but no more so than usual, for it was almost as if he had expected to see nothing but strange, sad things right from the day he was born. Carmine always asked them to take him away again almost as soon as they had brought him. One day, he said to Ninetta that, as soon as he was cured, they could think about their separation. It was a day when he felt quite well and death seemed far away. It was a day when they were alone. Ninetta nodded her assent, then went over to the window, not the one with the black lozenges, the other one, which just had a white curtain, and looked out over a yard. Ninetta was wearing a little pale blue open-work shawl. She pulled it tightly around her shoulders, pushed aside the curtain and rested her black fringe against the glass. He carried on talking about their separation, and said he thought separations should be peaceful and quiet and free from ill feelings. He said as soon as he was better, he would find a small place where Dodò could come and visit him on Saturdays and Sundays. Perhaps he would keep a little dog since she did not want to have one and Dodò loved dogs so much. Ninetta was still leaning against the window-pane, huddled even more tightly in her shawl. Suddenly, he became aware of the sound of his own voice, and never before, when he was with Ninetta, had he heard it sound so hoarse and squeaky and so alone. 'You're thinking I'm probably going to die,' he said, 'and that I'll never get a house or a dog.'

Then everything grew more and more confused inside his head. He never knew whether it was day or night, and he could never tell who was in the room and who had just left. Matteo Tramonti came every so often, and sat there, looking pale, in his short dark overcoat. He thought the fat lady lawyer came once, too, but he was not sure whether she had really come, or whether he had just imagined it. His parents were nearly always there, and so were Ninetta and Ivana. It seemed to him that Evelina came less often, and when she did come, she was minus the reassuring smile and the handkerchief, and bustled about the room in her fur coat, carrying boxes of hypodermic syringes, as if she no longer thought it necessary to smile or be reassuring.

Carmine now found himself gazing at his mother for long stretches, as she sat on the sofa in her black dress, and he remembered the times when they used to go to the neighbouring villages together, in search of bran for the pigs, because the war was on, and there was no bran to be found. He was a child then, and his mother was young. She had a full, pink face and white teeth. Her thick black hair was gathered into a fat bun studded with steel hairpins, and protruded from underneath her headscarf. He remembered one occasion when he was very tiny, still in his mother's arms, and they were in town, at the station. It was night time and pouring with rain. There were crowds of people with umbrellas waiting for the train, and mud was running between the tracks. Why on earth his memory should have squandered and destroyed so many days and so many events, and yet preserved that moment so accurately, bringing it safely through the years, tempests and ruins, he did not know. At that point, he could not remember anything about himself, what clothes and shoes he had worn, what wonder and curiosity had woven and unwoven itself in his thoughts at the time. His memory had thrown all that out as useless. Instead, he had retained a whole pile of random detailed impressions, that were hazy, but light as a feather. He had kept the memory of voices, mud, umbrellas, people, the night.

BORGHESIA

A WOMAN who had never kept any animals was given a cat. It was brought to her in a shoe-box with holes in the lid. At the same time, a tartan bag was put in her hand containing a bag of litter, a little yellow tray with a cat's head in relief, a bottle of vitamin pills and a phial of deodorant called April Breeze. She must return the tartan bag later, said the frail, gloomy old servant, who had appeared in her house as if from nowhere. Several evenings ago, as they were coming out of the cinema, Signora Devoto had told her that cats were a wonderful source of comfort, they spread a deep sense of stability, peace and calm. As soon as the cat was lifted out of the box, it darted into the living-room, ran up the curtains and stayed there, curled round the pelmet. It was incredibly tiny, biscuit-coloured, with a brown muzzle and paws and a short, curly tail. The servant told her it was a male Siamese, two and a half months old, and it was the son of Signora Devoto's mother's cat. He told her a cat should always have a basket to sleep in and a blanket, and for goodness sake, please give it water. He said the best food for a Siamese was rice and fish. The bones must be removed from the fish, and the rice should be very well cooked.

The woman was called Ilaria Boschivo. She had been a widow for several years. She was thin and wrinkled with short, woolly grey hair and big blue eyes. She lived alone. Her daughter and son-in-law lived in the flat next door, and her brother-in-law, Pietro Boschivo, in the flat above. Pietro Boschivo was an antiques dealer and provided for them all.

He was the brother of her late husband, Giovanni Boschivo, a theatrical impresario. A winding staircase separated his flat from hers. Her daughter and son-in-law, who were both eighteen, usually had their meals with her as they had no money and no desire to cook. The daughter was called Aurora and the son-in-law Aldo, his surname being Palermo. Ilaria and her old servant, Cettina, always did the cooking together. Cettina was tall and stooping, with a hooked nose. She had lived in Ilaria's house for many years. Her brother-in-law's servant ate there too. She was a short, stocky girl from Brindisi, called Ombretta, who had dark skin and a mass of curly hair. Ombretta never cooked, because she did not know how, and she never washed up either, because she had rheumatism in her hands, or so she said. Pietro Boschivo used to say she was useless to him and he kept her out of pity. Her family would send her out on the streets otherwise. She used to spend her days sunbathing on the upstairs terrace dressed in nothing but her slip, so as to get her thighs and shoulders brown. Then, in the evenings, she would go to the downstairs flat, where there was a television. She had her own room upstairs, but she always preferred to sleep downstairs in the guest room, where there was lovely flowery wallpaper and a painting of an old woman in a headscarf who reminded her of her grandmother. She used to leave her tattered old bras and stretched old girdles lying around in the various upstairs and downstairs bathrooms and, sometimes, a green towelling turban with a pearl in the middle. She always put this on in the mornings to do what she called her work, in other words, making her bed. It had been given to her as a present by a woman doctor with whom she had been in service for two weeks when she first came to Rome. She was always talking about those two weeks. She made them sound like a century. The woman doctor had been extremely fond of her, but unkind people had spoken ill of her.

Ilaria's bedroom had a bow window opening on to a small balcony. In the window, Ilaria arranged the yellow litter tray, the basket, the blanket and the water. Her daughter Aurora asked her why she did not put it all out on the balcony. Ilaria said she was afraid the cat would jump down below. She was happy to have it, but she was not sure what her brother-in-law would say. He used to come down the winding staircase at dinner times when he was not eating at the restaurant or at Signora Devoto's. He and Signora Devoto had a relationship that had been dragging on for years. However, even on days when he was eating elsewhere, he would come for half an hour, and sit down in an armchair at the bottom of the stairs and ask Cettina to bring him a lukewarm lime-flower tea. He would come down the staircase, a tall, frowning figure dressed in the same shabby purple jacket he wore winter and summer. He always inspected the room with his stern, black eyes, sniffed it almost, with his long, slender nose, then sat down, got the playing cards out of a drawer in the occasional table and played patience while he sipped his lime-flower tea. Then he went away again, calling out a brief casual goodbye from the top of the stairs. When the purple jacket had gone, and the head with its stern mouth and strong, white teeth, the room always seemed empty, frivolous and boring.

Ilaria knew her brother-in-law was not an animal lover at all. Besides, he had chosen her carpet and paid for it and had it put in for her, and he might say cats ruined carpets. This, in fact, was what he did say. He also said cats made carpets smelly and full of fleas, and that the carpet must be absolutely flea-ridden already. Ilaria said, as far as the smell was concerned, she had sprinkled April Breeze on the carpet. Pietro said he hated the smell of April Breeze, the Devotos used it, and he had begged them to stop doing so. Ombretta said she could feel the fleas jumping up her legs, and she stretched out a muscular, brown leg and a large grubby foot in a gold slipper. The woman doctor, the one she had been with for two weeks, had four cats, but they were angoras and did not have any fleas. Aurora said they must beat the carpet every day from now on. She was very lazy by nature, but she loved to plan great cleaning sessions.

To Ilaria's mind, neither peace nor calm emanated from that

cat, only worry and apprehension. It was a terribly nervous creature and used to dart and squirm about everywhere. It would hide under cupboards, then pounce on her head suddenly and rummage about and suck her hair. It seemed to know that of all the people in the world, she was the protector appointed to substitute for its mother, a distant feline figure whom it would never meet again. When she took the yellow tray into the kitchen to change the litter, it used to turn somersaults for joy, as if delighted someone was attending to its litter. Later on, it was the somersaults that stood out clearest in her memory when she thought of this cat. One night, it seemed to have a cold and a bit of a temperature. She thought it would die, it seemed too small to survive an illness. Next morning, she phoned Signora Devoto, who gave her the name and address of a vet. She wrapped the cat in a little tartan shawl and took it there. Whenever she thought of this particular cat afterwards, she thought of tartans: Signora Devoto's bag and the tartan shawl the day it had a temperature.

There were a lot of people with cats and dogs in the vet's waiting room. Several hours passed by. She spoke to a woman sitting near her, who had an enormous dog on a lead. 'This is the first time I've been here,' she said. 'Yes, I can tell you've never had an animal before,' said the woman. Ilaria was struck by this and wondered how the woman could tell. Perhaps it was the fact that her cat was wrapped in a shawl. Everyone else had theirs in suitable pagoda-shaped baskets, so convenient for travelling or for taking them to the vet. That day, she felt as if she had truly penetrated the circle of pet owners and animal lovers, a very special group of people united by a tenuous and yet extremely close bond.

This first cat had a very short life indeed. When Ilaria worked out afterwards how much time had passed since the day the servant appeared with the box and the bag, she realized it was scarcely more than two weeks. The cat recovered from the cold and began to dart and squirm about the house again, but then it died at home, accidentally. She had been to the supermarket with Ombretta, and they were on their way home loaded with heavy bags. When they got to the front door, they saw Aurora holding something wrapped up in news-paper. She threw it into the dustbin. 'Your cat's dead,' she said. Ilaria noticed, as she had done at other times in her life, that her daughter derived acute pleasure from bringing her bad news. She sat down on the stairs and started to cry. 'It was Uncle Pietro,' said Aurora, 'he didn't mean to. He just didn't see it.' Ilaria said she did not want to hear any more. The three of them took the lift upstairs, and Ombretta sang the cat's praises, saying how beautiful and intelligent it was, and how healthy and lively. While it was alive, she had found it a sickly, annoying little creature. When they got in, Aurora's husband, Aldo, was carrying some books downstairs with the help of Cettina. Pietro was sitting in the armchair looking pale. 'I'm terribly sorry,' he said. 'It wasn't my fault. I was carrying some books. I wanted to fill up these shelves of yours, they're so bare and I've got far too many books. Look, it's not my fault, I didn't see it. It's no good you staring at me like that.' 'It really wasn't his fault,' said Cettina. 'Why don't we go out and get another one? There are plenty of cats around. If you like, I'll bring you one straight away.' Aldo said perhaps they could send Ombretta to ask that woman doctor, the one with all the cats. 'Angoras they were,' said Ombretta. 'With no fleas,' said Aldo. 'They had all that lovely long hair, but it was so clean and never attracted fleas.'

Ilaria asked Aurora to phone Signora Devoto. She did not want to talk to another living soul about that cat. She went to her room and lay down on the bed. In the bow window, she saw the yellow tray, the green bowl full of water and the other bowl with some uneaten rice in it. Her mind stood still. A voice in her head kept repeating uselessly, over and over, 'cats die too you know'. She found it strange that so much pain radiated from those trays and bowls, because, as a child, she had been taught that animals did not matter, their presence in our life was meaningless and we should not suffer on their account. That was what she had been taught, and yet the face of that skinny cat was imprinted deeply and painfully in her mind's eye, where no one else could see it. He had wide, brown ears and a sharp, pointed, brown face with a lively but serious expression. It was one of the liveliest, and at the same time one of the most serious, faces she had ever seen. But behind that gravity, lay the greatest sense of fun in the world. To have lost him was a slight thing. It was a poor sort of pain. But, all of a sudden, she was discovering that even poor sorts of pain are acute and merciless, and quickly take their place in that immense, vague area of general unhappiness. Aurora came in and asked if she wanted her to close the shutters. She quickly took the bowls away, and then came back. 'It's all arranged with Rirí,' she said. 'She'll be coming round tomorrow morning.' Rirí was Signora Devoto. Her real name was Ginevra, but everyone called her Rirí. However, Pietro used to refer to her sternly and sarcastically as Ginevra. Perhaps he was the first person in the world to call her by that name.

Aurora sat by the bedside for a while. She was a tall, pale, slender girl with long hair that fell around her neck, moist, black and soft, like seaweed or grass. She was always doing something to her hair; combing it, touching it or winding it round her finger. She even chewed it. Ilaria had also had a son, but he had died of meningitis when he was nine. Aurora was eleven at the time, and the two of them had been left alone in the house, because the father was in a psychiatric clinic. They learned not to talk about painful things, and prudence became a habitual part of their relationship. Every syllable was weighed carefully so as to sound light and cheerful. When the father came home, all three of them went to Germany for a holiday, and the father talked of nothing but money, being desperately afraid of running out. In fact, they had run out of money, and it was a bitter trip altogether. Ilaria felt her daughter was developing a deep resentment against them both, thinking them stupid and unhappy and hating them for their unhappiness. After they got back, her father killed himself with sleeping tablets one day, after a quarrel with his brother Pietro over some land in Basilicata, which they owned jointly, and which Pietro refused to sell. So, Ilaria and her daughter were left alone in the house once again, with Pietro in the upstairs flat, and the land in Basilicata still unsold. All they got from it was a few bottles of bad wine from time to time. Almost immediately after her father's death, Aurora announced that she was marrying Aldo Palermo, a boy she had met at the sailing club. Aurora was studying political science at the University and, as for Aldo, he had dropped out of his studies and had some sort of vague plans. And, of course, they had no money. However, Ilaria knew her daughter's decisions were unshakeable. Aldo had black hair, almost as long as Aurora's, a large mouth that was always a bit sulky looking and a long, lean, supple body. His decisions were unshakeable too, and they were decisions that did not concern the future, only the present. They were not important decisions, but trivial ones such as making a cabinet out of rotting old boxes and then painting it blue and sticking transfers on it. His mother, who was a maths teacher, had already said she did not believe in this marriage and was not interested in it and did not want to know Aurora or her family. Pietro had always said the marriage was absolutely idiotic, but when he heard what Aldo's mother had said, he flew into a rage and went straight into an electrical shop and bought Aldo and Aurora an enormous fridge. Aldo and Aurora got married and moved, together with the fridge, into the flat next door to Ilaria's, which consisted of three rooms, a kitchen and balcony. It belonged to Pietro, just like the other two flats. The fridge stayed empty because Aldo and Aurora never bought any food. Aldo also had a father who was separated from his mother and did not give them any money. He was a doctor, and his only gesture was to present Aldo with a few medicine samples whenever they met in the street, and send him old shirts from time to time. Aldo never even put these on. He did not wear shirts. He always wore the same white cotton jumper with a roll collar, and when it started to smell too much, he used to wash it and lay it out, then sit and scratch his long, brown, sunken belly while he waited for it to dry. Aldo used to say his mother was a boring old pest, but not bad at heart.

He visited her once a week, partly because there was a dog at home that he loved very much. He came into the bedroom too that evening and told Ilaria he understood how she felt, because if anything were to happen to his dog Igor, he would be as upset as she was right then.

Next day, Rirí, that is Signora Devoto, came round and she and Ilaria went to get a new cat. 'When an animal dies,' said Rirí, 'you can and should replace it immediately.' Rirí was tall and stout with a wide face, small, pretty features, little white teeth and blonde hair gathered into a small bun on top of her head. She had broad hips and slim legs. She had already phoned a shop in via della Vite and the cat was waiting for them. It was a male Siamese, two or three months old. They walked there, striding all the way. Rirí was wearing a yellowish-grey fur coat flecked with white hairs. Ilaria had on a green knitted jacket, which Rirí said was too old and shapeless and not fit to be worn. Rirí thought Ilaria should ask Pietro to buy her a fur coat, but Ilaria said she did not like asking Pietro for things because they all lived at his expense.

Rirí said Pietro had given her the money for the cat the evening before, after she had explained to him that you could buy Siamese cats. In Rome, it cost 50,000 lire to buy a Siamese cat in a pet shop. Pietro had remarked that cats were rather expensive. He was in a strange, sad mood and sat and played poker with her husband and children and hardly said a word all evening. Pietro was curt and brusque, said Rirí, but he had a kind, sensitive soul, and although he pretended to be hard and strong, inside he was as frail as a leaf. Anyway, he had been strange and sad for some time now, and she knew why. He had fallen for a nineteen-year-old girl and he wanted to marry her. Pietro was one of those people who get very miserable when they are in love. The girl lived at Camilluccia and came from a rich family. Her father owned a building firm. She was a tiny slip of a girl, like a little nun. Ilaria asked in what way she was like a nun. Rirí said she was, really. She was cold and hardly ever laughed, she was one of those girls who always keep their lips pressed tightly together and never look you in the eyes. 'It doesn't matter to me if he marries her,' she said. 'I haven't felt anything for him for a long time. But it will be horrible for you. He won't give you money any more. He'll only think of himself. The little nun will have goodness knows how many children. You'll be ruined if he marries her.' 'I don't care,' said Ilaria. 'I'll learn to work. None of us work. Aurora can learn to and so can Aldo.' Then Rirí told her once again what she was always telling her. She must persuade Pietro to sell this famous land in Basilicata, ask him for her share, and then buy a little house by the seaside or in the country and live on her own. That way, she would be able to dedicate herself to her art. In her youth, Ilaria had written a novel entitled *Gianmaria*, which had had a certain measure of success. But after that, she had stopped writing. If she took it up again she might be successful and earn a lot of money. 'Just imagine living in the country with a lovely cat, and some dogs. I'd come and see you every Saturday. I might even take a cottage nearby.' Rirí felt Ilaria was trapped in the family circle and she would do well to break away. They did not treat her well at all. They were parasites. Even Pietro was a parasite to some extent, despite the fact that he gave her money generously. She was the one who kept house for him, ironed his shirts, cleaned the spots off his suits and put his blankets in mothballs. He had taken on that girl Ombretta who was absolutely useless. 'And I'm surrounded by parasites too,' she said. Rirí had four children and an elderly husband and they were such a burden. Her days were so heavy, there were dinners and suppers to be cooked and that lot all asking her to do everything at once. Where's my jumper? Look up the train timetable for me. Take me to the station. Do up the zip of my windcheater. We're going to have a party on the terrace and we need twenty pizzas and fourteen bottles of coke and will you put the wine in the fridge. She had her servant, but he was completely unreliable. He resigned every week and they had to beg him to stay and take him to have acupuncture because he suffered from insomnia. For a number of years, seven to be exact, she had enjoyed a close relationship with Pietro, and it had been an amazing source of consolation to her. But it was over now, and had been for some time. Pietro came to their house out of habit, to play poker or Chinese checkers with the children. 'Us poor women,' she said. 'They drain us. They walk all over us. They never look at us for years on end, and then they're surprised, one day, to find we've got wrinkles and tired eyes and lifeless hair.' 'You haven't got lifeless hair,' said Ilaria. Riri stroked her bun. 'It doesn't show very much because I put it up like this. But it is lifeless. When I let it down at night and run my hands through it, it pains me to feel it.'

The new cat was different from the old one, in that it was fat with thick hair and had a long tail. But it was the same colour and had the same large ears and serious expression. It was in a cage with another, identical, cat who was its sister, so the shopkeeper said. For a moment, Ilaria was tempted to take them both. But she needed another fifty thousand lire. Anyway, Riri dissuaded her. She could have two cats or as many cats as she liked when she moved to the country. Riri had brought along a braided bag lined with woollen rags, and the cat was placed in it. When they got it home, it ran off and hid underneath a settle, where it stayed all night. Early next morning, it was sitting quietly on the divan in the living-room, and Cettina and Ombretta said it was a much nicer cat than the other one, not at all silly or nervous. Ilaria called it Fur, because of its thick coat and because Riri had been wearing a fur coat the day they went to collect it. The first cat had died without a name.

Fur lived with her for a year. At first she found him lacking in personality, a bit stupid perhaps, and incapable of deep affection. But after a while, she discovered that, for Fur too, she was the most important person in the whole world. She realized that, in his eyes, she was the only person of real value. He would follow her all over the house, and curl up on her clothes; on the knitted jacket she always left on the settle and the stockings and underclothes she left lying on the bathroom floor for Cettina to wash. This feeling of being valued so by a cat filled her with a strange sort of pride. It was a pride that seemed rather pathetic and stupid to her sometimes; hardly worth dwelling on really. After Fur had been with her for a few days, she felt he might be torn with regret over his identical twin sister who had been left behind in the cage in the shop. She went back there with the idea of buying her, or at least seeing her again, but the shopkeeper said she had been sold. Ilaria would have liked to ask him where he got his cats and which house Fur was born in and what kind of people lived there. But she did not dare ask him anything, his manner was brusque and not very pleasant. It was sad to think she would never know anything about Fur's birth or the place where he had come into the world. It was a strange, poor sort of sadness. She thought to herself how everything that bound people to animals and animals to people was strange, poor, sad and mysterious.

One day, Ilaria had been to the cinema with Rirí and asked Rirí to come upstairs because she wanted to show her a suit she had bought. Ombretta came out to meet them and said Fur was very ill. They found him lying in Cettina's lap, shivering, his back covered in blood. Cettina said he was in agony. Ombretta and Cettina told her he had followed them out on to the terrace when they went up there to hang out the sheets, and while he was out there, on the roof, they had seen him fighting with an enormous tabby cat. Or rather, the tabby cat had jumped on him and bitten him. Pietro appeared; so did Aldo and Aurora, and they all made helpful suggestions such as boric acid, cold compresses and compresses with tincture of iodine. Rirí phoned a vet she knew and begged him to come at once. The vet came, and said he did not really want to give a definite prognosis, not because of the wound on Fur's neck, but because some internal organs had been damaged. However, it was possible he might live. After the vet had gone, they all sat in the living-room. They had brought the cat in with them, in his basket. 'What a shame,' said Pietro. 'He was such a nice cat. I really liked him. He'd almost converted me.' 'We're really unlucky with cats,' said Aurora. They were talking as if Fur was already dead. 'Stop reciting the funeral oration,' said Rirí. 'He's more alive than anyone else in this room. He'll outlive all of us.' 'Ginevra's an optimist,' said Pietro. 'I can't bear you calling me Ginevra,' she retorted. 'My name's Rirí.' 'And I can't bear your optimism,' said Pietro. 'That cat's going to die.' Ilaria started to cry. 'You beast,' said Rirí to Pietro. Ombretta came in and said the tabby cat was still hanging around the terrace, and it was frightening, it had a really fierce face.

For a few days, Fur stayed in his basket, and Rirí came to give him injections and feed him with an eye-dropper. He seemed engrossed in the effort of staying alive. He lay very still with his paws drawn in, emanating an air of immense gravity. They had found out from the caretaker that the tabby cat was called Napoleon and belonged to a lady jeweller. For some unknown reason Napoleon had taken it into his head to be absolute master of that particular part of the roof. Cettina and Ombretta said he was still there, lying in ambush near the guttering, looking grim and fierce. Rirí and Ilaria went out on to the terrace to look. Ombretta threw a bucket of cold water over him, but he did not move. Rirí scolded her. She said it was a cruel thing to do. She suggested they phone the lady jeweller and ask her to come and collect him. Ilaria had already lumped Napoleon and the lady jeweller together in her mind, in a single fervent hatred. However, the jeweller came and Ilaria stopped hating her immediately because she was a pleasant, meek, likeable person. She apologized for the trouble her cat had caused. 'He's caused more than trouble,' said Rirí. 'He's caused a lot of fear and unhappiness.' Napoleon was still there, wet and ugly looking, clinging to the edge of the roof. 'Nappi,' murmured the lady jeweller, gently. Nappi came to her, and she took him away wrapped up in her apron.

After a week, Fur had recovered. They could tell he was better when he got out of his basket and went to the water bowl. The vet had told them always to leave it near him; but in any case, Ilaria had remembered the words of Rirí's servant that evening a long time ago. For goodness sake, please give it water. The servant had fled to Switzerland in the meantime, having been involved in an obscene photographs scandal. For a while, Ilaria was afraid Napoleon would come back, and the thought crossed her mind that if he did, she would grab him and put him in a taxi, then take him to the other side of town, to Eur or Villa Borghese, where he would not be able to find his way home. But she told herself this was a cruel scheme. The lady jeweller would wait in vain for her Nappi, and Nappi might end up under a car as he roamed the back streets in despair. Nappi did not come back, however. The caretaker told her both he and the jeweller had left for the seaside. The summer passed. It was a long summer that year, and Ilaria and Fur were left alone because everyone else had gone away on holiday. Cettina and Ombretta had gone home to their respective villages. Aurora and Aldo had gone to Iran with some money Pietro had given them, and no one knew where Pietro had gone. No doubt he was in Umbria with the little nun. Umbria was where her parents went in the summer. They had a house there. Rirí told Ilaria all this over the phone from Chianciano, where she was taking the waters. They were a rich family, she said, and had houses and villas all over the place. The little nun went riding; she loved horses, and dogs too, she was crazy about animals.

Pietro was the first to come back. He did not say where he had been, but he brought two enormous jars of home-made fig jam. It remained a mystery whose home they had been made in though. Ilaria did not ask him about his holidays; she made a point of never questioning him. He was very sad and hardly spoke at all. In the meantime, Fur had grown into a big, fat, strong cat with a dark coat. 'He's not dead,' said Pietro, every time he saw him. 'He really looked as if he was going to die that night.' At last, one evening, he told her he was getting married. He said it in a very low voice, sitting in his usual chair at the foot of the winding staircase. Fur had jumped on to his knee and he was stroking him with his strong, beautiful white hand. He murmured that she was a very young girl and he was almost certainly making a grave mistake marrying her.

He found her youth fascinating, but at the same time, repugnant. It was a cold, indifferent, silent sort of youth. He did not understand her, and he was marrying her in order to be able to understand her. Ilaria said, but would it not be better to understand her first, then marry her? He replied that he could not tell any more what was for the best and what was for the worst. He was very confused. He could not think any more, he just felt anxious and miserable all the time. He stroked the cat's long tail. 'She likes cats,' he said, 'and dogs, all animals in fact. She's very good at horse-riding. She's even won some competitions. She's got cups and medals. She's one of those people who always wins. We might move. She doesn't like winding staircases or attics, she prefers the ground floor. I shall have to find a ground-floor flat with a garden, because she loves trees and countryside and town gardens. Or rather, she thinks she loves gardens, but she doesn't really love anything except herself.'

He said Aldo and Aurora could come and live in his flat and let the three rooms they were living in. His was an excellent flat and had that splendid roof-top terrace where you could grow flowers and make shady corners and bowers. You could even have a swimming-pool. The Devotos' terrace was smaller than his and they had managed to grow real dwarf trees there. It was so cool, just like being in a wood. They had never wanted to put in a swimming-pool; although goodness knows why! There were certain kinds of plastic swimming-pools you could buy very cheaply. Aurora and Aldo were bound to have children one day. They would really enjoy themselves in a swimming-pool, and there would be no need to spend money on summer holidays. It was so expensive to go on holiday these days that, more and more, people were tending to organize themselves to as to be able to stay in town right through the summer. That splendid terrace of his was no use to anyone at the moment, except for Ombretta to sunbathe on and for Napoleon to massacre poor Fur to within an inch of his life. They went up on to the terrace together and sat in the two rickety armchairs where Ombretta and Cettina sometimes used to sit and chat. 'Can you feel how beautifully cool it is?' said Pietro. 'It's criminal to have a beautiful terrace like this and not keep a single plant on it. Tomorrow I'll go out and buy an umbrella so that I can come and sit out here in the afternoons.' Fur had followed them up and was rolling on the floor, rubbing against the empty flower-pots lined up along the surrounding wall. He jumped on to the roof and Ilaria called him. He came to her. 'You're obsessed with that cat,' said Pietro. 'It's impossible to talk to you any more, you're always thinking about the cat. You've become a real cat fanatic.'

Cettina came back bringing a suitcase full of pears from her village. They were green and rock hard. For a while they stayed green and sour, then, suddenly, turned brown and went rotten. Ilaria and Cettina laid them out in the kitchen on some newspaper. Cettina said where she came from they were called angels' pears and they were used for making jam. The kitchen filled up with ants and, in the end, Cettina picked up the whole squashy mess, ants, pears, newspapers and all, and threw it away. Ombretta was not coming back. She had sent Cettina a letter from Brindisi saying she might not be back because she had met a woman journalist in a bar who wanted to employ her as a secretary and was going to take her on a long journey. A postcard arrived from Forte dei Marmi, with a picture of beach umbrellas. Ombretta had written on it: 'Wonderful spot.' They heard nothing more. Cettina said she did not know what to do with all those clothes of Ombretta's that were still hanging in the wardrobe in the guest room. She said they worried her; they were a responsibility.

Halfway through September, Aldo came back alone. Aurora was in Greece with some friends. She was well and did not intend to come home for the time being. For the next few days, Aldo just slept. He came to meals, with his cotton jumper all creased and dirty, and went back to his flat to sleep as soon as he had eaten. Next, he started making puppets. He had met a young man in Teheran who earned money from making puppets. So now he spent his days in the kitchen sawing up old boxes he had found in his mother's attic and taken back to the flat on his motor bike. When he had sawn them all up and piled up the various pieces of wood in one corner of the kitchen, he asked Ilaria for some money to buy paint, and for some scraps of material. He decided to call his first puppet Mustapha. Mustapha was painted green. He had a fat, square face and a large mouth with permanently gnashing teeth. He was dressed in a long green robe made out of a piece of leftover material from one of Ilaria's dressing-gowns and decorated with seed pearls. More puppets followed and they all had square faces and big mouths with gnashing teeth. Then Aurora came home looking slim and suntanned. She had bought herself a long tunic in Teheran, with a pattern of stars on it. She told Ilaria that she and Aldo had decided to separate. She had fallen in love with someone else during the trip. She sat down in the living-room and said this a few hours after she got back, twisting her hair round her finger as she spoke. Her hair was rather dirty. She said she had not washed it for weeks. Ilaria started to cry, and Aurora told her there was nothing to cry about; she was very happy and felt very clear in herself about the whole thing, and as for Aldo, he respected the importance of her feelings and was not unhappy. The essential thing in life, said Aurora, was to refuse unhappiness with clenched teeth. There were three things in life you should always refuse to take: hypocrisy, resignation and unhappiness. The night she had first made love to Emmanuele, she had woken Aldo and told him immediately. 'Who is this Emmanuele?' asked Ilaria wearily. 'Emmanuele is a wonderful person,' said Aurora, 'I'll introduce you to him. He's studying the philosophy of language.'

It was difficult for Ilaria to tell Pietro and Cettina that Aldo and Aurora were separating. She expected them to react to the news with exclamations of surprise. Until that summer, Aldo and Aurora had always been seen with their arms round each other. Now Aurora was out all day; she did not even come in for dinner, and Aldo was absorbed in his puppets. He appeared at dinner times, as ever, and sat down calmly at the table, as if nothing had happened. His thick-lipped, pouting mouth simply looked slightly sulkier than usual and there were a few scarcely discernible wrinkles among the bushy hair, bathed in sweat, that cascaded about his forehead. Neither Pietro nor Cettina seemed particularly surprised. Cettina said, 'Well, these things happen: marriages and separations. I've heard Pietro Boschivo is getting married. That's a good thing. Aurora and Aldo got married too young and that was a bad thing.' Pietro said, 'What a pity. I know Aldo wasn't much. He hadn't found his way in life. Still, it's a shame.' He spoke of Aldo as if he were dead or far away. But, no, Aldo was still there in the flat next door with his puppets. He had started to move some of his things by motor bike; books and the various gadgets he needed for his puppet-making. He had found a room in via dei Serpenti which he intended to share with a friend. But he was taking things bit by bit, two or three books at a time, a couple of things here and there. He was in no hurry. Besides, the room was not ready yet, his friend was still whitewashing the walls. He had stopped coming to Ilaria's for meals because Aurora had told him there was no point in him eating there any more. Instead, he went to a restaurant at the corner of the street. Cettina would see him in there when she went by, and she said it upset her, because it was sad to see him perched, like a chicken, on one of those high stools, with a plate of cold, soggy chicory in front of him. Cettina was always passing the restaurant and she knew what their food was like. She thought it looked like the most awful muck.

Rirí came back from the spa. She came to see Ilaria immediately. She knew all about Aldo and Aurora already because Pietro had told her what had happened over the phone. Rirí was the only one who said she was surprised and sorry. She kissed Ilaria and consoled her with caresses. Ilaria felt a more acute pain, but a sense of relief at the same time. Rirí was the only person she could talk to about this separation in the same way as she talked to herself. She remembered the evening she had sat on the terrace with Pietro and he had talked

to her about Aldo and Aurora's future children who would
have a little plastic swimming-pool there, where they could
play with toy boats and rubber rings. That evening seemed
hopelessly long ago, and yet it could not have been much
more than a month. Rirí knew Emmanuele, because Rirí
always knew everyone. She said he was a crazy, scatterbrained
boy, and not good looking at all; in fact he was ugly and fat.
The word 'wonderful' was going round and round in Ilaria's
head at that time, partly because she remembered the postcard
from Ombretta that said 'wonderful spot', and partly because
Aurora had called Emmanuele wonderful. Consequently, she
could not imagine him being as ugly and fat as Rirí said he
was. Rirí knew how to tell fortunes from tarot cards. She had
read the tarot cards for Aurora and had seen the prison, the
hanged man and the monk. These meant solitude and chastity;
but at the end there was the sun. She had also read the cards
for Ilaria. Ilaria had the falling tower, which meant ruin, and
then the pope's throne, which meant success and power. Still,
said Rirí, it was more important then ever that she should
think about retiring to the country, and trying to make a life
of her own far away from Aurora and Pietro and all their
eccentricities. Pietro would be getting married in a few weeks'
time, and he planned to move, but she knew he would stay
where he was, and then Ilaria would be forced to play the
servant to the little nun and everyone else besides. Rirí had
seen the little nun in the street. She had on a checked jacket
and baggy trousers, and Rirí had thought her pretty, but a
bit stunted and green looking. Her hair was nice and she had
a slightly turned-up nose, but extremely bandy legs.

Rirí asked Ilaria if she wanted a female kitten. There was a
female kitten in her mother's house; a half-sister of the first
cat who had died in such an awful way. She was several months
old now and would make a wife for Fur before long. Besides,
Ilaria needed the affection of a kitten to console her. Fur was
randy and yowled all day and night. Ilaria used to open the
terrace door for him, on the advice of Cettina, and he wandered over the roof-tops in search of females, and they had to

shout themselves hoarse calling him before he would come in. It came to their ears, via the porter, that Fur was spending his time on the lady jeweller's terrace now, in the company of Napoleon. They had become intimate friends, Fur and Nappi. Ilaria remembered Nappi clinging to the guttering, wet through and looking grim and ferocious. She remembered the time when she hated him and had planned to take him to Villa Borghese and leave him there. Ombretta was with them then. Aldo and Aurora always had their arms round each other. She thought they would have children.

Rirí arrived with the kitten inside a wicker basket. It was an extremely thin kitten with a short curly tail, and looked very much like the first cat that had died without a name. It had a quiet temperament, however, and sat down on the sofa as soon as it was let out of the basket, just as if it had known the house for a very long time. Rirí said this was a wonderful kitten. Her name was Lulla, because she liked to sleep so much. Fur did not like the new kitten and hissed in her face. After she came, he stayed out on the roof-tops more than ever. She was too young, and therefore useless to him, and he judged her presence to be an intrusion. Ilaria used to go out on the terrace and call him. One day, she was out there calling him and she saw him on a roof-top in the distance; a small figure wearing the yellow flea-collar she had bought him on the advice of Cettina. The yellow flea-collar disappeared over a wall. 'Please come back. Good cat!' murmured Ilaria. 'Oh, please come back.' 'Fanatic!' said Pietro. He had bought himself an umbrella, just as he had said he would, and a new deck-chair too, and he was sitting underneath the umbrella typing on that hot autumn afternoon. He was writing his childhood memoirs. He had written fifteen chapters already. Ilaria waited for Fur until dusk, then she went back downstairs because she had to get the supper ready. Domitilla, in other words the little nun, was coming to supper and she would be meeting her for the first time.

The little nun came, bringing a guitar. She played the guitar very well and Pietro wanted Ilaria to hear her. He said it was particularly lovely to hear her sing and play 'Borghesia'. She sang while they were waiting for supper. The song went: 'Vecchia piccola borghesia / per piccina che tu sia / io non so se mi fai piu rabbia, pena, schifo o malinconia.' [Although you are so small, petit bourgeois of old, I can't tell what I feel most for you: anger, grief, disgust or melancholy.] She had a thin voice, raw and shrill. Her hair was wild; a huge, shiny mass of kinky golden waves. She was delicate looking and had a snub nose. Her legs really were very bandy and she wore an enormous pair of boots. Perhaps it was precisely because she looked so emaciated and undernourished that she was so pretty. Her hands looked tiny against the guitar strings and had a greenish pallor. They were the hands of a dwarf or a small child. 'What a little midget,' said Aurora, as she chatted with Ilaria while they were carving the roast. 'She can't really be in love with Pietro at all. Perhaps she's marrying him to get away from home. She seems cold and snobbish and I don't like her at all with those boots and that guitar.' However, Pietro seemed fascinated by the guitar and he was miserable and anxious and very much on edge. He got angry over the roast, which he thought was dry, and the potatoes, which he said were burnt on one side and raw on the other. Ilaria found it strange to see him in love. She had always seen him with Riri before, and when he was with her he seemed bored, stern and distant, and never noticed what he was eating. That evening, Pietro said he was probably going to buy a beautiful two-storey house in via Cassia. It had very large grounds and the branches of the tree brushed right up against the windows. He wanted to go up on the terrace to show Domitilla, who hated attics so much, how nice they could in fact be. But, in the meantime, a furious storm had broken, with thunder and lightning and hail, and Domitilla carried on playing and singing until very late while she waited for the rain to ease. Ilaria was thinking of Fur out wandering on the roof-tops.

Fur never came back, and Ilaria found out later that she had seen him for the last time that moment on the terrace while Pietro was typing and she had watched him disappear among the chimney-pots some way away. The porter told her there were two dead cats lying in a yard nearby. They had fallen off the roof. One was Fur and the other was Signora Macrì's cat. Signora Macrì was the wife of a diplomat who lived in an attic overlooking that very yard. The porter said the cats had probably fallen while they were making love. Cats lost their sense of balance when they made love, he said, and they might have fallen the night of that terrible storm when there was a really high wind blowing and there was thunder and lightning. Ilaria never wanted to go and look out over that yard, even though both the porter and Signora Macrì offered to let her. She continued to scan the roof-tops from her terrace, hoping they would bring Fur back to her alive, wearing his yellow collar, the usual serious expression on his broad face and his tail held aloft and quivering. 'Ch'ella mi creda libero e lontano' sang Pietro, 'e sopra une nuova via di redenzione,' and these words were constantly on Ilaria's mind during that period. She connected them with a vision of roof-tops, chimney-pots and gutters. Pietro had immediately said Fur must be dead when he did not reappear. 'Poor old fanatic, she's really unlucky with cats,' were the words he used one day when he was drinking coffee with Aurora and Cettina. The lady jeweller also gave Ilaria her condolences when they met one day in the small local market. She had a window overlooking that yard too, and she had recognized Fur because he was such a good friend of Nappi. She had had Nappi doctored when he was a kitten; and it was a good thing, she said, because it can be very dangerous up on the roofs. Cats lose their heads when they mate and become completely disorientated.

Winter passed once again and spring came, and Pietro was still planning to get married but kept putting it off because Domitilla had to study, or practise for a horse-show or play in a folk-group. Rirí had a house in Consuma, in Tuscany, and she invited Ilaria to spend a few days there. So Ilaria left Lulla in Cettina's care with a fervent plea never to let her out on the terrace. When she got home, Cettina was in a terrible rage because Aurora had taken Lulla to a villa at the gates of

Rome, where a friend of hers was staying, and where there was an un–neutered tom cat; and now Lulla had run away and they could not find her anywhere. Aurora appeared and said she was sorry, but Ilaria only had to come to the villa and call Lulla herself. Lulla would recognize her voice and come immediately. Nothing could be simpler. Ilaria and Aurora went to the villa together. Ilaria disliked Aurora's friend instantly; she had an affected air of boredom about her, and did not even offer her a cup of coffee. She was staying at the villa as a babysitter and had been left in charge of several children while their mother was on holiday. They were very dirty-looking children and she did not seem to bother with them at all. There was a big field of poppies in front of the villa, and Aurora told Ilaria the cat had run off in that direction. Ilaria spent the whole morning calling Lulla, Lulla, as loudly as she could and feeling really stupid, while Aurora and her friend sat at the edge of the field chatting to each other. Later, when she thought back on that morning, Ilaria could not help feeling poppy fields were unlucky places, vast and empty, and incapable of restoring cats to their rightful owners. A bit like roofs really. Aurora told Ilaria they must go now because her friend had to cook the dinner. It was a long afternoon, which Ilaria spent with Rirí and Aurora. Rirí tried to console her, and Aurora said they must make a sign of the cross over Lulla from now on. They both said Aurora was a real cretin. Ilaria thought of Lulla's habit of shaking a paw in disgust when her food was too hot, and realized she was thinking about her more and more as if she were dead. The poor cat must have felt so abandoned and betrayed as she fled into the poppy field. She must have felt utter contempt for her, and the very thought tore her apart with grief. Rirí suggested they might put up some notices in the area around the poppy field: 'Lost, Siamese cat with a curly tail. Generous reward offered', then the name, Boschivo, and the address. Late in the afternoon, Aurora's unpleasant friend phoned and said she had heard a cat had turned up in a villa nearby. However, she could not go herself because she had fallen out with the people who lived there.

Rirí, Aurora and Ilaria went together in Rirí's car, and rang the bell at a door which said 'Marchese Paradiso'. It was opened by an elderly gentleman in slippers and pyjamas. He seemed surprised and annoyed. However, Rirí informed him immediately that a certain Paradiso family were great friends of a cousin of hers called Puccio Paglia, and a brief but pleasant conversation on the subject of Puccio Paglia ensued. The elderly gentleman said, yes, there was a cat in his garage. It had managed to get into a hole in the wall, and they could hear it miaowing inside the wall. He kindly provided them with a handful of biscuits and they went into the garage. 'Lulla, Lulla, come on!' murmured Ilaria, standing in front of the hole in the wall. 'Come on, lovely girl, out you come.' At last, they managed to seize Lulla by the tail and pull her out. She was covered in chalk-dust and half crazed with fear. Pietro was there when they got home, and he told Aurora if she ever touched any of her mother's cats again, he would simply throttle her. Lulla had run straight to the water bowl and was gulping down water like mad, scarcely pausing for breath. After that, she fell asleep from sheer exhaustion, and slept for the rest of the day. Rirí told Ilaria she should send Marchese Paradiso a big bunch of red roses. She had found out in the meantime that he was a homosexual, very rich and very mean, and his wife had run away from him.

Aurora said she was going to live in the country with Emmanuele, in a house near Viterbo that some friends of his had just left. It had no electricity or water, but it was set in splendid countryside. Aurora asked Pietro for some money to pay the first year's rent, but she said she would not ask him for anything from now on because she and Emmanuele would write plots for cartoon romances, and anyway, they could live on nothing in the country. The house had a garden where they could grow salad stuff and tomatoes. Ilaria said she wanted to meet this Emmanuele at least once. Aurora brought him to her. Emmanuele was fat and pallid with a thick, mousey beard and a tight, black velvet jacket done up with a single button across his fat stomach. Underneath this jacket, he wore a yellow artificial silk smock. Ilaria could not make him out at all because he hardly spoke a word the entire time he was with her in the sitting-room. He simply held Lulla in his arm and stroked her tail with his effeminate-looking hand, which had a large, ornate ring on the little finger. While he was sitting there, Aurora was in the flat next door packing her cases. The hours went by and Ilaria did her best to engage Emmanuele in conversation by asking him a few hesitant questions, but he replied in monosyllables all the time; still stroking the cat and whispering in her ear. Then Aurora came back with the cases, and she and Emmanuele carried them downstairs. Looking out the window, Ilaria saw they were loading them onto a Volkswagen with battered mudguards, and just at that moment, Aldo arrived and helped them to tie one of the cases on to the roof rack with a piece of rope.

Aurora left for good a few days later. A van came, and she had the fridge loaded into it, together with a writing-desk and a dinner service that had never been used. Aldo was still living in the flat, and Pietro told Ilaria she should ask him, very delicately, to leave, because the flat could be let. But Ilaria knew from talking to Cettina that Aldo had not found a room yet. He had told Cettina that the room where he had taken some of his things, the one he had been going to share with a friend, had fallen through. Still, Ilaria went to see him. She found him sawing up boxes for his puppets, bare from the waist upwards, while the cotton jumper hung on the balcony to dry. He greeted her pleasantly, and Ilaria thought to herself that he was better than Emmanuele, nicer and a bit more communicative. He told her he was having some success with his puppets and might be able to set up a small theatre in a basement, together with some friends. The theatre would be called Mustapha. He assured her he would go as soon as he could find somewhere to live. He had heard about an excellent little flat in Testaccio, but he had to wait for the landlord to evict a tenant who did not pay the rent. Ilaria begged Pietro to be patient. She felt sorry for poor Aldo and she still thought of the times when he and Aurora had seemed so close and so happy. Aurora had even taken the fridge with her, so Aldo could not even drink a bottle of chilled mineral water when he was thirsty.

One day, Ilaria had a phone call from a nun. This nun said that in the hospital where she did night duty, there was a poor sick girl asking if a Signora Boschivo would come and visit her. The girl's name was Maria Ombra Conci. Ilaria could not think who it might be; then she suddenly realized it was Ombretta. She went to the hospital. She did not recognize Ombretta at first; she had bleached her hair and her head was now a mass of yellow curls. She was sitting on a bed in one of the wards, wearing a padded turquoise dressing-gown. She threw herself around Ilaria's neck, sobbing, then blew her nose hard into a handkerchief that smelled of eau de cologne, and said she had been at death's door. It was all that woman journalist's fault. She had given her to understand she was going to take her on as a secretary, but had then sent her to live in with some cousins of hers, as a servant. There were at least ten people in that house, and, one night, she was hot and sweaty and they had ordered her to carry some crates of wine down to the cellar. Consequently, during the night she had developed a high temperature, with vomiting and stomach pains and they had had to rush her to the hospital in Florence. She had had an operation and they had kept her in for two months. Then she had found a job in a bar in Florence, where she had met a highly respectable accountant who had taken her to his family's house in Rome. They had eaten squid roasted on a spit for supper one evening, and this had made her ill. Either the squid were not very fresh, or there was too much pepper on them. She had fainted at the table, and the accountant had taken her to the casualty department, because she had also started haemorrhaging terribly. It had frightened him to see her covered in all that blood, and he had come to visit her once, but had told her he would not marry her because she was not too healthy. But she had always been very healthy. They would remember how healthy she had been before she had landed up in Florence. They could vouch for the fact that she had sound liver and lungs and everything else for that matter. She asked Ilaria for a bit of money to buy oranges and cigarettes, because she had not a single lira left in her purse. She opened up her purse, and inside was a telephone token and a sweet. The journalist's cousins owed her two months' wages, and she had left a lovely new pink woollen jacket there too.

Ilaria spoke to the Sister in charge of the ward, who told her that, certainly, Maria Ombra Conci had had peritonitis in the past, but this time she had had her womb scraped because of a miscarriage, and, in fact, this was an obstetrics ward. A week later, Ombretta dropped in at their house, restored to good health, wearing black bell-bottom trousers and a yellow top. She said she had come for her clothes, but as soon as she had sat down in the kitchen, she burst into tears and begged them to let her stay there for a few days because she had absolutely nowhere to go. A little later, Pietro came in and told her she could stay permanently if she liked, provided she was not going to be quite as useless as before. So Ombretta settled into the guest room again, and for the first few days, she was up at dawn, cleaning windows, ironing and cooking fiddly dishes that took ages to prepare, because, she said, she had learned to cook a little in the meantime. Then she got tired of it all and returned to her old habits of sleeping in late and waking up bleary eyed and dopey, and sunbathing on the terrace, and everyone breathed a sigh of relief because the dishes she had been cooking were absolutely awful.

Rirí said it had been a mistake to take her back again, because she would certainly cause trouble. But Cettina said they had done the right thing because Ombretta was good-hearted, and with a bit of patient supervision, she might even develop a wonderful touch around the house. Above all, they had done the right thing because otherwise, she would only become a prostitute in the end. For the first few days, Ombretta was constantly bombarding Ilaria with questions. Was she absolutely sure Fur was dead? Where was Aurora, and why didn't Aldo come for meals any more? Was it true that Pietro was getting married to a little girl, who was not at all good-looking, but was a millionairess, and her name was Petronilla or something? She cried over Fur. She cried over the breakdown of Aurora's marriage and the fact that Aldo was alone. She was amazed at Pietro's forthcoming marriage and cried over that too. However, she said, she had plenty of tears to spare. She had had a bad time all these months, being ill-treated and humiliated in that wretched house with those cousins of the woman journalist, and she had even been close to death.

Lulla had grown up in the meantime. She was a long cat now, and had dark fur. Ilaria loved her more than ever since the day she thought she had lost her in the poppy field. She would sometimes think how the years accumulate on a cat too, so that every time you saw it walk by silently at your feet, the burdensome memory of everything that had happened to you went by with it. She used to wonder whether Lulla was unhappy there, with just them, and no other cat to keep her company. She felt cats must get so bored in the company of people. It was summer again. Ilaria was not left on her own this time, because nobody budged. Pietro had his house in via Cassia to think about, and Cettina did not want to go on holiday, because, she said, she felt too old and tired to face any journeys. As for Ombretta, she was going to a beautician's every day to learn about make-up; so she was out in the mornings, but in the afternoons, she was at home practising putting on beauty-masks; so sometimes she would appear with her face covered in a sort of chalky blue crust. There were still no flowers or trees on the terrace. There was just the umbrella, and it was impossible to sit under it because it was so hot, and the sun was unbearable. So Pietro used to wait until evening, then go up there and type, taking a tilley lamp with him. The little nun would come about that time too, bringing her guitar. Ilaria and Rirí still called her 'the little nun', but Ilaria could not really understand why they had got into the habit of calling her that. She used to sit on the ground holding her guitar, with her head resting on Pietro's knee, while he stroked her thick, golden mane of hair;

a bit more absent-mindedly these days than he used to. She sang 'Borghesia'. He had loved that so much at one time, but it bored him now. 'Vecchia piccola borghesia / per piccina che tu sia / non so dire se fai piu rabbia, pens schifo o malinconia,' sang Ombretta, in chorus, as she went about the house in her sun-dress, her face covered in that blue, chalky crust.

Pietro's marriage lasted seven months. The wedding was a big affair, with a reception at the Hilton Hotel. It was in September. Ilaria had a long, brown silk dress made specially. Aurora came up from the country with Emmanuele. Ilaria had already been to visit her five or six times, but always when Emmanuele was away, because Aurora said Emmanuele had a difficult relationship with his own mother, and therefore could not cope with other people's mothers. Aurora was pregnant. The day of Pietro's wedding, she wore a red velvet maternity dress. It was too tight, too short and covered in cats' hairs, because she had three cats and two dogs in the country. The cats were not Siamese, they were feral cats gathered from the countryside. Their names were Night, Day and Dusk. The dogs were called Paul and Julius. They were two huge mongrels, the size of cows. Aurora had explained to Ilaria that they did not keep their cats in the same way as she kept hers. First of all, they let them run completely free, and secondly, they were not obsessed with them like she was, and they were not always worrying about them. Sometimes they even forgot to feed them. But for all that, they were healthy. Emmanuele had sat himself down in a corner, wearing his usual tight velvet jacket, and was drinking whisky. He did not exchange a single word with anyone. He said 'Hi' to Ilaria and barely touched her hand. His own hand was as soft as ever. Then he turned his back on her immediately. He had a problem with mothers, said Aurora. Ilaria did not like the house in the country where Aurora and Emmanuele were living, at all. It was a sort of vast, dirty barn in the middle of a sunny, deserted plain, with not a single tree in sight. She did not like Emmanuele either. Aldo was at the wedding too, sitting in a corner some way off, and he also stayed there on his own, drinking and saying nothing. Pietro had thought it would be a nice thing to invite him. Pietro still hoped he would leave the flat, but he liked him better now than when he was living with Aurora. Theirs had been such a senseless marriage, and it might not have improved Aurora, but it had improved Aldo, and it had woken him up a bit. Grief and humiliation sometimes do that to people, said Pietro. Those puppets were really ugly though. Rirí was there, looking radiant, because she had decided she must look as radiant as ever at Pietro's wedding. So she had put on a dress with a pattern of big red roses, and wore a real red rose in her hair, and thought herself much better looking than that green-faced little creature in her gypsy skirt and lace blouse, which was, of course, too elegant for the skirt, and her mass of splendid, but completely unkempt hair, and her button nose and tiny, pale mouth that always looked a bit sulky, like Aldo's. All the little nun's family were there. They were terrible people, said Rirí to Ilaria; millionaires and tax dodgers. The little nun was playing the rebel. She could not be more than one metre fifty-five in high heels, and she was wearing heels that day. Usually she wore boots, and they made her look like Puss in Boots. But it was too much of a compliment to compare her with a cat. Fortunately, the house in via Cassia was in Pietro's name. For a moment, he had thought of putting it in her name, but his guardian angel had given him a tap on the shoulder.

Pietro and the little nun left for their honeymoon in Holland, both of them taking their typewriters, because Pietro wanted to carry on writing his memoirs, and the little nun wanted to continue with a thesis she was writing, on Caravaggio.

Pietro and the little nun never went to live in the house in via Cassia. When they got back from their honeymoon, they settled in the upstairs flat. For the first few days, Ilaria asked them if they wanted to have their meals with her. The little nun thanked her and said yes, and said they would get themselves organized later, and Ombretta would learn to cook eventually. In the end, Ilaria just cooked for them without even bothering to ask. At first they had spent some time in via Cassia with a friend of Pietro's, who was an architect, in order to plan new bathrooms, curtains and carpets. Then they said the friend was on holiday, and they stopped going there. Rirí said she thought the marriage was tottering already. They probably did not get on well together in bed. Pietro often came and sat in his usual chair at the bottom of the staircase. He did not play patience. He did not type. He had told Ilaria he had come to a halt with his memoirs. He sat there in the chair for hours on end, doing nothing, just smoking and stroking his chin and cheeks and hair. The little nun always got up late. Sometimes, they could hear her shrill voice from upstairs, singing *Borghesia*. Ombretta used to say, 'It's the only song she knows.' Relations between Ombretta and the little nun were not good. The little nun had told Ombretta she had sagging breasts, and if she did not do something about it quickly, they would hang down to her thighs by the time she was thirty.

Pietro's shirts and the little nun's dresses were ironed by Ilaria, in the downstairs flat. Cettina never did any ironing because she was always tired and could not stand for very long, and Ombretta never did any ironing either, because, as she put it, she was a bit afraid of irons. 'So, you're more or less their servant,' said Rirí. 'That was easy to predict.' At table, Ilaria, Pietro and the little nun made polite conversation about light-hearted, cold topics such as the food, certain of the little nun's relatives whom Ilaria had met at the wedding and who were now useful as a subject of conversation, the food again, the curtains for the house in via Cassia, which had already been bought, but were perhaps too dark, Caravaggio, and so on. Aldo came one evening to ask for a screwdriver. Pietro greeted him with pleasure and asked him to stay for supper. Then Aldo saw the guitar. He knew how to play too. Aldo and the little nun sang together, taking it in turns to accompany one another. Naturally, one of the songs they sang was *Borghesia*. There was an open fire burning, because the little nun adored open fires. Pietro was raking about in the grate. Ilaria was knitting for Aurora's baby, who was due to be born soon. Lulla was asleep. Ombretta and Cettina were listening by the door. It felt like a peaceful evening to Ilaria, unlike most evenings, which seemed peaceful on the surface, but were full of hidden tensions. She thought to herself that it was Aldo's presence making everyone feel better. Pietro said afterwards he thought Aldo was nice. It was hard to tell why he was so nice, because he never said anything out of the ordinary, but he had a soft, light-hearted, kind approach to life. Pietro said he could even stay in the flat for good, because, if he left, they might get someone really dreadful in, who did not pay the rent. Aldo did not pay any rent, but perhaps he would later on, when he started to earn some money from his puppets. He was not in a position to at the moment; all he had was a little money his mother gave him.

The little nun started to go regularly to the flat next door to play the guitar with Aldo and watch him while he made puppets, or washed his cotton jumper or made himself dinners of milk, cheese and eggs all mixed up together. He had stopped going to the restaurant. She helped him to paint his puppets and stick long, red moustaches on them, made of thread. She liked them. She did not find them ugly at all. Aldo's dog Igor, who was a big wolfhound, was staying with him at the time, because his mother was in a clinic, where she had had an operation for a stomach ulcer. The little nun used to take Igor for walks. Ilaria would see her tiny figure from the window, with her boots and her little snub nose red with cold as she was dragged along by that enormous dog.

Rirí came to supper one evening, along with her eldest son, a boy with red cheeks like two pieces of steak. She had brought a pheasant, which her son had caught and she had cooked. While they were eating it, the little nun said she was against game hunting. It was horrible to shoot poor little birds. So Rirí and her son got into an argument with the little nun, and Pietro said he was against game hunting too, and Rirí told them they were all very rude, because she had spent so much time and trouble that afternoon cooking the pheasant in red wine, and her son had got absolutely soaked through with rain shooting it. After that there were long silences. Rirí said she had a terrible headache. Her son said nothing and sat with his hands between his knees. The little nun had started to sew up the hem on a skirt as soon as supper was over. Aldo and Pietro were playing chess. Rirí phoned Ilaria next day and said it had been a horrible evening, and she could not stand that Aldo either, with his cotton jumper and the way he had of swinging his chair back and scratching his head and shoulders. Pietro said to Ilaria would she please not invite Ginevra again, or that son of hers, who was an absolute idiot, because he did not feel up to coping with them at the moment, amongst other things, he was depressed for various reasons, which he did not explain. Ilaria was thinking to herself that, for years, he had spent his evenings in Rirí's flat, eating pheasants and playing ping pong and Chinese checkers with her children. But she said nothing, because she did not want to provoke him, and because she had got out of the habit of telling people what she thought some time ago.

That winter, Lulla gave birth. She only had one kitten, which they called Solitaire. It died almost immediately. Lulla had been mated with the butcher's cat, a big Siamese, who was shy and moody and did not seem to desire female cats, and hid under cupboards.

Aldo and the little nun ran off together one day. It was the thirtieth of December. Ilaria was at the clinic with Aurora, who had just had a baby girl. She came home early in the morning, feeling exhausted, having spent the whole night standing up in the hospital waiting-room, next to Emmanuele, who was doing crosswords and drinking beer. Every so often, he offered her some beer in a paper cup, and asked her a question about the crossword when he was stuck. That beer, that paper cup and those questions were the only small signs of kindness he had ever shown her. When she got home, Ilaria found Pietro sitting alone in his usual chair. He had a sweater on over his pyjamas, and he was fiddling about in the fireplace with a poker. Ilaria did not dare ask him where the little nun was. She started talking about the baby. He asked a few questions about the baby, but that was all. Then he showed her a letter, or rather, a few lines scribbled on a page from a notebook. 'I'll send my parents' chauffeur to collect my clothes. Domitilla.' 'She's gone away with Aldo,' said Pietro. 'They'd been going to bed together for a month or two. Ombretta told me. She found them together and came to tell me. She was going to bed with Aldo too, so she had a key to the flat. When Domitilla came in, I asked her if it was true that she had been going to bed with Aldo. She said, yes, it was true, she had, for a month or two, she couldn't remember exactly. She said it was not important to her, but she was not happy with me. She didn't know why she had married me. I slapped her face. She stood there looking as calm and pale as before and started to put her boots on. Then she went out and came back again. She told me she and Aldo were going to Circeo. Her parents had a villa there. She asked me if I wanted to say goodbye to Aldo, but I didn't. I didn't even want to hit him. I came and sat down here, and I've been here all night. I could hear her moving about upstairs, but then I fell asleep. It seems strange to me that I fell asleep, but I really did. It was like falling into a dark pit. When I woke up, I heard the sound of a motor bike in the street outside. It was dawn. I saw them leave together on the motor bike. She had a rucksack on her back. The dog was gone. I don't know what they've done with it.' Soon after that, the porter came to see them and said the dog was with him. Aldo had said please would he look after it for a few hours. He had tied it up in his office with a piece of rope, but it had started barking now; perhaps it was hungry. Ilaria gave him a parcel of leftovers. Then the chauffeur came, a stocky little man. He took the suitcases of clothes that were ready, done up and waiting in the upstairs bedroom, and the guitar. He said he also had orders to collect a dog called Igor from the porter.

Cettina told Ilaria that Ombretta was in a very bad state. She was lying on the bed in the guest-room sobbing. She said she had aches and pains everywhere, in her stomach and her belly and her chest. She said she would never have peace of mind again, for the rest of her life, because she would always remember that awful moment. She had gone to Aldo's flat to take him a bottle of Asti Spumante and a fruit-cake that she and Cettina had bought him. They felt sorry for him because he was spending Christmas and the New Year alone. She had found the dog in the hall and those two in the bedroom, so she had slipped away quietly, at once, with only one thought in her mind, to tell the doctor, the doctor being Pietro. He had turned so pale. He looked like death. That girl was a little slut. She was spiteful too. She had once told her her breasts were like two fat aubergines. She was just jealous, because her own breasts were like dried-up crab-apples. Cettina came in with a cup of soup, but Ombretta said she did not feel like eating or drinking anything, her stomach felt as if it was on fire. On the floor near the door was a bottle of Asti Spumante and a large fruit-cake done up in a red cardboard box with gold stars on it.

Ilaria never saw Aldo or the little nun again. Aldo wrote to Cettina asking her to send the things he had left in the flat to his mother's house. Cettina could not read, so Ilaria read the letter to her. It was just a few hastily scribbled lines, with best wishes to everyone at the end. Ilaria and Cettina went into the flat next door and gathered up into a box the five or six puppets that were still lying around, plus the saw and a few scattered rags. There was very little in the way of clothing, just a windcheater, a pair of jeans folded in four and a pair of muddy boots. He wrote again, thanking them. The first letter came from Circeo, the second came from London. Pietro met the little nun's parents in a lawyer's office and they began proceedings for separation by mutual consent. Aurora and Aldo, for their part, had never bothered going to any lawyers, and so Aurora's baby daughter was given Aldo's surname of Palermo for the time being, until Aldo did something about officially denying paternity.

Then Pietro went away with Rirí to her house in Consuma, in Tuscany. He stayed there for a month. When he came back, he looked tanned and healthy, having had a complete rest and taken some very long walks. Rirí said she had tried to persuade him to sell the famous land in Basilicata, which was now worth a lot of money because it had a building licence attached. However, she had not succeeded. It was useless, he just did not want to sell and it was impossible to tell why. Instead, he sold the house in via Cassia, in a great hurry and lost money on it, at least twenty million lire, said Rirí. He was left with yards and yards of curtain material, which he kept in a cupboard in his bedroom. In the end, Rirí bought it for her mother.

Pietro told Ilaria to dismiss Ombretta because every time he saw her he thought about the bottle of Asti and the fruit-cake, and her presence was disagreeable to him. However, in the meantime, Ombretta had taken to her bed with renal colic, and they would have to wait until she was well again before they could ask her to leave.

Then Cettina died in her sleep. Early one morning, Ombretta had gone into the room at the far end of the hall where Cettina slept, and had let out a tremendous scream. At the funeral were Ilaria, Pietro and Rirí, and a niece of Cettina's who was a baker. Ombretta stayed at home because she was ill. She was now saying she wanted to leave, because everywhere she went in the house, she saw Cettina's tall, stooping figure, with her woollen slippers and black apron, and her long nose.

Ilaria phoned Rirí and asked if she could find Ombretta a position somewhere. Rirí sent her to her sister-in-law's house, where they made her put on a brown overall with a white piqué collar, and taught her to wait at table. However, she only stayed there two weeks, then disappeared and was never heard of again.

Ilaria and Pietro were alone in the house now, or rather, in their separate homes, with Lulla the cat. Lulla had been mated with the butcher's timid tom cat again, and was pregnant once more. Pietro and Ilaria had never been able to talk to each other very much, and they were still unable to do so. Pietro apologized now when he gave her his shirts to iron, because

Cettina was not there any more. He either did not know, or had forgotten, that Cettina never ironed shirts. They never spoke of Aldo or the little nun. It was almost as if they had never existed. Ilaria knew that when they had returned from London, they had gone to live in a farmhouse in Cerveteri that her parents had bought for them, and they were rearing horses there. She heard this from Rirí, who always knew everything that was going on. Aurora wrote to Aldo in Cerveteri, asking him to do something about denying paternity. She was pregnant again. Aldo replied promising he would do something about it, but he was very busy with the horses right now. He had given up making puppets. He had said goodbye to all that. His letter was just a few hastily scribbled but affectionate lines.

Aurora came up from the country one day and asked Pietro for some money. Emmanuele had bought the house near Viterbo, with a loan from a friend, and now they had to pay back a certain amount each month. Pietro said he had very little money at the moment. It was a bad time for the antique business. Aurora implored him to sell the land in Basilicata. Pietro said he did not want to sell it; at least for the time being. They quarrelled, and Aurora went away furiously angry. Pietro ran down the stairs after her and brought her back. Ilaria cried, and they made it up. Aurora said Emmanuele was writing a book and a publisher had promised him an advance. Pietro said he hoped to conclude a deal with a cousin of Rirí's, called Puccio Paglia, and if he succeeded, then all would be well again.

Aurora had another little girl. She wanted to have the baby in the hospital in Viterbo this time. Ilaria went to Viterbo, then went back with Aurora to the house with no electricity or water, which Emmanuele had bought for some unknown reason. They took a taxi from the hospital, because Aurora did not feel like driving; she was still tired after the birth, and Emmanuele was not there. He had gone to Mexico to get some information for the book he was writing. The elder daughter had been entrusted to some neighbours, along with the two dogs and the three cats. Aurora went to collect them all. The house was dirty, and Ilaria set about cleaning it from top to bottom. She said it would take days to clean it properly. They would need to buy a few pieces of furniture too. There was only one cupboard, and everyone's clothes had been chucked into it, along with all the plates and saucepans and blankets. The floors were made of terracotta. They would have to swill them with buckets of hot water. To get the water, they had to go to the stream.

Looking out of the window while she was washing the floor, Ilaria saw Aurora sitting in the front yard of the house, breastfeeding. There was no shade, so Aurora had put on a large beach-hat. The older daughter was playing in her pen, and the three cats and two dogs were sniffing about nearby. However, before Ilaria had completely finished cleaning the house, Aurora told her she had better go, partly because she was tiring herself too much, and partly because Emmanuele was due back, and, as she was always saying, he had a problem with mothers.

When she got back to Rome, Ilaria found Rirí in the flat, helping out Pietro. She had got a big cardboard box from the chemist's and lined it with scraps of woollen material, and put it in the bow window in Ilaria's room. It was for Lulla, who was about to have her kittens. Rirí said cats will quite happily have their kittens in a box. She pointed out that Aurora and Lulla always seemed to give birth about the same time.

That evening, while she was with Rirí and Pietro, Ilaria started to cry, and said she thought Aurora was unhappy. She thought it outrageous that Emmanuele had gone off to Mexico just when Aurora was about to have her baby. Rirí and Pietro tried to console her. Pietro said he had almost concluded that deal with Rirí's cousin, Puccio Paglia, and would soon be able to send Aurora some money to improve her house and make it a bit more comfortable. But Ilaria replied that Aurora would be unhappy even in the most comfortable of houses. Rirí said Aurora seemed to have the knack of finding the wrong men.

Aldo was no better than Emmanuele. You might even say he was infinitely worse. Pietro then asked them to be so tactful as to refrain from talking about Aldo in front of him. He did not want to be reminded. He had never wanted to let or sell the flat next door. It was still empty. Rirí said Pietro could not write his memoirs if he did not want to be reminded. Pietro said that, in fact, he had come to a halt with his memoirs some while back. He only wanted to remember tranquil, harmless, light-hearted things.

A few days later, Lulla gave birth to five kittens. She did not have them in the box though, she had them in Ilaria's bed. It was during the night, and so Ilaria lay asleep, surrounded by tiny kittens that looked like white mice.

In the morning, she picked them up gently, one by one, and put them in the box. Lulla squeezed herself in beside them and stayed there for weeks suckling them. Every so often she got up and turned to gaze at Ilaria, her face tired, serious, calm and sad.

Then the kittens started to dart about the house. They could drink milk from a saucer now, and they ate fish with rice. Sometimes Pietro would find them upstairs in the bathrooms, or even in his bed. He had learned to be patient, and said he was not against cats any more. He did think there were too many of them though. Perhaps they could take them to that shop in via della Vite and sell them. But Ilaria did not want to. She did not like to think of them shut up in those nasty cages. They might be there for a long time too. When they were three months old, she would give them away, and take great care to see that they went to people who would love them.

One day, Ilaria fainted while she was crossing the street. She was taken home by a traffic policeman and the lady jeweller, the one who owned Napoleon, and who just happened to be passing at the time. When they arrived, Pietro asked them to put Ilaria to bed. Then he called Rirí. 'I've called our Ginevra,' he said, 'she's such a gem when anyone's ill.' Rirí came with a doctor. Ilaria was taken into a clinic. Then began a long series of tests that lasted for weeks. Ilaria had cancer of the left lung. No one said anything to her, but she knew she was very ill and thought she would die soon. Pietro and Rirí kept her company. Rirí said she was going every day to attend to the flat and all those beautiful cats. Cats were an immense source of comfort, she said and so were dogs. Pietro then begged them not to talk to him about dogs, because he did not want to be reminded of Igor, the wolfhound.

Aurora came. She had stopped breastfeeding already, and the baby was drinking cow's milk that came fresh, every morning, from the farmer's wife. She had left both babies with a friend, and besides, there were the neighbours too. Ilaria pointed out that they were only neighbours in a manner of speaking, because it took half an hour's walk along a stony road to get to them. But, anyway, wasn't Emmanuele there, she asked. Aurora said Emmanuele had had to go away again. He was meeting his publisher. She did not say that, to tell the truth, Emmanuele had come back from Mexico and told her he was leaving because he had another woman, and she did not say that they were deeply in debt, and she was dreadfully tired of living in the country and did not know what the hell to do about it.

Ilaria told Rirí to look after Lulla when she was dead, and give the kittens away. Rirí told her not to talk rot. There was nothing wrong with her. She only had a little fluid in the lungs. Perhaps they would do a small operation on her. Ilaria said she could not explain why, but lately, whenever she looked at Lulla, it made her think about dying. She felt it might be due to a faculty for guiding her thoughts into unknown realms. And, anyway, quite apart from that, she had started to think about dying from the moment Rirí had sent her that first little cat in a shoe-box. Words became so loaded with memories as the years went by, and because of that, they became full of weariness and pain. Now, every time she said the word 'button' she thought about the little nun, with her button nose. Goodness knows how Pietro managed to remember nothing but tranquil, light-hearted things. Wherever could you find something tranquil? Aurora said nothing. She sat and chewed her hair and wound it round her finger. She remembered saying that there were three things in life you should always refuse: hypocrisy, resignation and unhappiness. But it was impossible to shield yourself from those three things. Life was full of them and there was no holding them back. They were too strong and too cunning for mere humans. 'Please stop putting your hair in your mouth,' said Ilaria. Aurora was filled with an overwhelming desire to tell her about the night Emmanuele had come back and said he was leaving her. How he had gone away again after three days, and during those three days, they had somehow found themselves exchanging a barrage of angry, hateful words, and suddenly putting on a hypocritical air of politeness and calm when the children, or the farmer's wife, or the neighbours were there. But she said nothing, and endeavoured, all day, to be brusque and cool and calm with her mother, so that she would think everything was as normal. She did not even tell Rirí and Pietro. She thought to herself that unhappiness was not only a very complicated thing to talk about, it was humiliating too. Aurora went back to her mother's flat, to have a bath and rest a bit. She stopped for a moment on the landing, in front of the flat next door where she had once lived with Aldo. On the wall beside the door, she and Aldo had written 'Palermo' in Indian ink, with a drawing of a flower. Her two daughters were called Palermo because Aldo had not yet denied paternity. In the hallway of her mother's flat, the kittens, with their wide brown ears and sharp pointed faces, were sitting waiting in the gravest possible silence.

Ilaria died during the night. Aurora came to the clinic at Pietro's call, but when she arrived, Ilaria was already dead. Aurora and Pietro hugged one another tightly. Rirí came, and cried. Rirí's relatives and children, the porter and the lady jeweller all came in the morning.

After the funeral, Rirí helped Aurora to sort out Ilaria's clothes and belongings. In a cupboard, she found all the school exercise books belonging to the son who had died when he was nine. They also found a lot of copies of the novel *Gian-maria*. In the kitchen, in the housekeeping accounts book, they found a photograph of Ombretta on the terrace, wearing a sun-dress and a sombrero, with Fur, the cat, draped round her neck. Aurora said she wanted to take Lulla and the kittens with her. They reminded her of Ilaria. Later, when the kittens were three months old, she would give them away to the neighbours and the farmer's wife. Rirí came again next day and helped Aurora to get all the cats into a basket she had bought specially. It was pagoda-shaped, with a little opening, like a window, for them to look out of; so convenient for taking them to the vet or on journeys, said Rirí. Aurora had come in the old Volkswagen with the battered mudguards. The basket was placed carefully on the seat, which was covered in sweet-papers and biscuit crumbs. Rirí spoke out in praise of Volkswagens. Pietro said, quite right, they were excellent cars, as solid as tanks. Aurora agreed. She did not say that the Volkswagen really belonged to Emmanuele and he wanted it back. She got in, and Pietro and Rirí watched her leave. She glanced back at them for an instant, Rirí with her black headscarf tied underneath her chin, her hands in the pockets of her mac, and Pietro, with his shabby purple jacket, his delicate grey head held high, and his dry, stern eyes.

AFTERWORD

A man and a woman went to see a film one summer Sunday afternoon.

NATALIA GINZBURG published enough writing about film to fill a short book. Short—but powerful, because she didn't write film reviews or film theory but, rather, personal essays about her experience of seeing particular films. "After writing," she declared, "cinema is what incites my curiosity and interests me the most." In 1977 alone—the same year she wrote the novellas *Family* and *Borghesia* over the summer and fall and saw them in print by November—she published essays about Federico Fellini's *Casanova*, *Andy Warhol's Bad*, and Éric Rohmer's *The Marquise of O*.

Ginzburg evokes herself as a filmgoer using language that echoes her very occasional reflections on her own writing, the best known of which, "My Vocation," describes literary creation as a practice "which ... swallows the best and the worst in our lives and our evil feelings flow in its blood just as much as our benevolent feelings." In an essay from the mid-1970s, she uses a similar set of dialectical terms: "I love cinema with the best and worst parts of myself: I love it expecting the benefits of truth, beauty, and knowledge, and also as a way of satisfying my meddlesome, lazy, gossipy, and reprehensible thirst for falsehood." Both writing and filmgoing evidently require one's humanity with all its contrary impulses.

In her film writing, Ginzburg relies on her usual feint as an essayist—"I don't want to imply that I have any knowledge of films. My

impressions are just those of an ordinary member of the audience"—
and then goes on to write exquisite prose poems about Pier Paolo Paso-
lini's *Salò* and Fellini's *Satyricon*. Ginzburg really disliked Marco
Ferreri's *Dillinger Is Dead* and other '60s art films that held up frag-
mentation and ennui as a mirror to their audience. In response to such
films, she wrote: "The dreariness of living cannot be expressed unless
life is loved and regarded with passion and surprise"—a maxim to keep
in mind when you read these two novellas, which are pervaded by the
dreariness of living.

Nota bene: I'm not leading up to a claim that Ginzburg has a cine-
matic method or that her fiction has a filmic quality. In fact, Ginzburg
herself asserted:

Often, I think about the difference between writing and making
films; it seems to me that making films is a way of telling a story.
But this is a false notion. Films do not tell a story because the
temporal dimension is absent in cinema. Narrative or—more
precisely and in terms of genre—poetry uses verb tenses, the imperfect and the distant past, as its essential tools; while a filmmaker lacks such tools. A filmmaker deals with stories about
people, just like a novelist; but a filmmaker does so without the
temporal dimension. The great joy of expressing oneself by saying, "I was," "I had," "I will think," and "I asked" is a joy denied
to those who paint pictures, to those who compose music, and
denied, despite appearances, also to those who make films.

I'm not sure that many artists working in these mediums would agree
that they lack the means to explore temporality, but neither would I
dismiss a writer who translated most of *Swann's Way* into Italian during the final years of Mussolini's regime when she reflects on her own
ways of getting "the temporal dimension" into fiction.

Ginzburg's novel *Voices in the Evening* (1961) features so much dialogue that it's almost a shooting script, but *Family* and *Borghesia* each

resemble a treatment; that is, the summary of a script's narrative. When I first read these novellas thirty years ago, in my initial encounter with Ginzburg's fiction, I was enthralled but also confused by them, because their narratives felt both rushed and crammed with detail. Quoting from the novellas proves difficult because even short passages refer to multiple characters, whose interconnections one must map out. Summary often replaces dialogue but, occasionally, a pointed individual utterance—a good line, so to speak—rises above the hum: "I don't care a fuck about aubergines in oil."

Most of the paragraphs begin with the kinds of time markers we use when relating a chronological sequence of events: "Next day... At last... Then, suddenly... During the months that followed ..." Sometimes the syntax laconically juxtaposes endings and beginnings: "Pietro's marriage lasted seven months. The wedding was a big affair, with a reception at the Hilton Hotel." The novellas' characters often grasp at specific moments in the past; to embody this impulse, Ginzburg uses the past-perfect tense almost obsessively: forward then backward, forward then backward. Consider this sentence about a cat's fate: "Fur never came back, and Ilaria found out later that she *had* seen him for the last time that moment on the terrace while Pietro was typing and she *had* watched him disappear among the chimney-pots some way away" (my italics). For Ilaria, who misses her lost cat, only in retrospect does the moment commemorate an actual disappearance, and that retrospective viewpoint ("later") becomes the novella's "now."

The language of ongoing disappearance—the act of watching something vanish before it's completely gone—pervades both novellas: "Ninetta spent her days lying on the bed, looking pale, and staring vacantly into space watching her adultery fade into nothing." All of these dissolutions and endings culminate in the deaths of the novellas' focal characters—"Carmine lived for another two months"; "Aurora came to the clinic at Pietro's call, but when she arrived, Ilaria was already dead"—each death narrated with an absence of fanfare, as just one more ending among the many endings that occur within time, like the ending of *Abyss*, a movie about millionaires and sharks through which a few characters sit impatiently in *Family*.

"I do go to the movies all the time," Ginzburg once told an interviewer. The critic Cesare Baldoni thought theater far superior to cinema as a genre and said as much in a 1975 polemic. Ginzburg responded, not by coming to the defense of film by praising Ingmar Bergman or Fellini, directors whose work she revered, but by exploring her ambivalence about watching trashy movies, name-checking only a soft-core porn comedy and a romantic Western starring Burt Reynolds:

> When I go to the movies, I know very well that I can't constantly demand truth, knowledge, and beauty, and, in general, I am resigned to not finding them except on a rare and most unusual occasion. When I go to the movies, I know I will sit in the dark and watch horrors. For example, it's summer at the moment and few films are playing in the city; we have to choose between *Esotika Erotika Psicotika* or *The Man Who Loved Cat Dancing*. Their titles, and the summaries one reads in the newspapers, reveal the quality of what we'll see. I will wait for buckets of trash and dirty water to be thrown in my face—since this is what bad films are; and why is it that someone like me, who loves good films, has left home and sits there in the dark until the end, unable to get up and leave even when tedium and a kind of anguish caused by that tedium pour down from the screen? Why? I would be glad if someone explained it to me since I don't understand it and I don't know.

She does not suggest one obvious answer for going to see *The Man Who Loved Cat Dancing* in the summertime in Rome—namely, the air-conditioned movie theater. However, that is why, in Ginzburg's *Family*, Carmine and Ivana, two close friends who once were lovers, take their respective children, and the child of a neighbor, to the movies.

The theater's air conditioner turns out to be broken, and when the moviegoers, including Ivana's teenage daughter, debate in whispers about whether or not to leave, a confusion of pronouns ensues: "Angelica said they were mad; they had paid five thousand lire for the tickets. Someone in the row behind went shh! The millionaires were in a speedboat, ploughing through a swirling blue sea, throwing spray high in the air all around them. They died one by one, some of them killed by each other and the rest eaten by a shark. It was still afternoon when they came out of the cinema."

The characters' desultory afternoon at the movies and their hours-long sojourn at a café, which serves as a narrative frame in *Family*, becomes, in the retelling, the unattainable past. The novella's title hints at what lies in that past: an ever-receding sense of belonging—or of having once belonged. Carmine and Ivana form the novella's central dyad not because they might fall in love again but because "they had so many memories in common." Those memories, which include the birth of a daughter who "died of infantile paralysis when she was one and a half years old," form the unspoken basis of their present bond. At Ivana and Angelica's apartment, Carmine creates an alternate family life for himself, away from his wife, Ninetta, and their son, Dodò:

Carmine got into the habit of coming quite often. Ivana sat and worked at her translations, and he sometimes looked up words in the dictionary for her while he played chess with Angelica or lay on the settee and read the paper. About midnight, he would phone Ninetta to say he was coming home soon. Ninetta would send a big kiss to Ivana and Angelica. But he would still stay stretched out on the sofa for a while, reading, smoking and looking out of the window at the trees along the road, the bridge, the river and the roof-tops bathed in moonlight. When they were alone, they usually talked about the present: Ninetta, Angelica and Dodò. They rarely talked of the time when they had lived together. To both of them it seemed like a strange, remote era when they had got the absurd idea into their heads that they could live together, even though they were so different and had opposite and irreconcilable characters. They sometimes remembered Fidel, the cat, with affection, but they never spoke of their dead daughter.

Ginzburg lamented the "breakdown of families" in Italy of the 1960s and '70s as "an affliction of our times." Yet the makeshift, sometimes temporary families her characters create in these two novellas and in her subsequent novel, *The City and the House* (1983), seem, at times, almost free of the constrictions and inherited obligations that characterize families in her earlier fiction. If that very freedom brings its own complications, and even tragic burdens, the characters can escape them, however momentarily—as Carmine puts off returning to the performative affection of his wife's "big kiss."

One of the deepest moments of closeness in *Family* occurs when Carmine comforts Ivana after her on-again, off-again lover, Amos Elia, has killed himself: "Carmine was holding both her hands, and stroking them. They were thin, pale, nervous hands. He *had* known them for a very long time" (my italics). Even such a short passage—a single sentence in Italian, "*Carmine le teneva le mani e gliele accarezzava, erano mani magre, pallide, nervose, egli le conosceva da tanto tempo*"—uses past perfect to create a sense of temporal depth: Ivana's hands in the present merge with the hands Carmine first knew when they were lovers, more than a decade before.

Carmine isn't the only character in these two novellas who searches for an alternate family. In fact, Ivana describes Carmine's own ex-lover, the twenty-something Olga, as "a girl who's . . . looking for mothers, fathers and brothers. Then she gets bored. The ones she's found seem wrong for her. She feels she's landed up in the wrong place, so she looks for another." I suspect Olga exemplifies the rootlessness Ginzburg saw and lamented in young Italians of the 1960s and '70s. (The baby-faced vagabond dilettantes of *Borghesia* are suffused with sadness in a way that the characters approaching middle age in *Family*, who have experienced adult griefs, are not.) However, Carmine and Ivana's relationship endures precisely because of its status, as Lynne Sharon Schwartz observes, as "a family of the kind that keeps recurring in [Ginzburg's] later fiction: arbitrary and ephemeral, replacing the traditional prewar family." For Carmine, Ivana and her daughter become "the people with whom he felt best in the world. It was easy to be with them." And later: "he found himself thinking that the best part of his existence was Ivana and all that surrounded her. No other source gave him that vital something which made him more intelligent, less ordinary and stronger."

In the time-bound world of Ginzburg's fiction, however, this experience of ease and vitality must come to an end. On the night he sickens with what will turn out to be a fatal illness, Carmine remembers times when he ventured out of the upper-class milieu of his marriage to bum around Rome with Ivana and her friends: "He was assailed by an acute nostalgia for the evenings he had spent in that theatre, those uncomfortable seats and dusty boards decked out with red curtains. It seemed to him that those evenings, and others he remembered spending with Matteo Tramonti and Ivana in the streets, cafés and piazzas, were part of a remote, lost era." (Here Ginzburg may recall her own past as a translator of such passages from Proust as "these Combray streets exist in so remote a corner of my memory.") The word "nostalgia" recurs when Ivana visits Carmine in the hospital, their conversation shadowed by a shared, unspoken awareness of his impending death:

Ivana said they had talked so quietly together that Sunday at the café. Carmine said that, now, thinking back on that Sunday, it seemed like a very nice day, and yet, he had not noticed it at the time, because there was nothing wonderful about going to see a bad film, nor about sitting in a café, ordering ice-creams and waiting for the evening to come. He felt an agonizing nostalgia for that day now, and yet, they had been bored sitting in that café, thinking they would spend thousands more days like that one, just as they had done in the past, because there was nothing so easy and mindless as sitting in a café for a few hours.

Carmine's longing for that "boring" day recalls Ginzburg's perplexity about why she would sit through an awful movie "even when tedium and a kind of anguish caused by that tedium pour down from the screen." In *Family*, she answers that question by framing her narrative around what turns out to be Carmine's last visit to a cinema, although no one in the novella makes so dramatic a statement. Carmine's experience gains significance, in retrospect, precisely because it seemed tedious at the time. Ginzburg's characters often describe themselves as "bored," but, as she wrote in an essay from the 1960s, "boredom does not exclude happiness. They can coexist, and can join together, inextricably tangled."

That entanglement gives Ginzburg's fiction its sense of closeness to what we call real life, in which the notion of discrete emotions functions as a consolatory fiction amidst the disarray—on every possible level—of our daily existence. Italo Calvino summons that disarray when he asserts that Ginzburg's "simple, elementary sentences… nonetheless manage to contain a relationship with the outside world made of affection, dismay, irony, the recognition of the limitations of the self and everyone else, the repetitions of gestures, of hours, of life's flux, of *an ever-possible and ever-fleeting happiness*" (my italics). At the end of his own sentence, Calvino not only describes Ginzburg's vision of experience as ever-changing; he also imitates her way of embodying "life's flux" in language. In all of her writing, Ginzburg pairs apparently opposed terms or contrary impulses in a dialectical manner, to suggest paradox and simultaneity: "a real home, both reassuring and inimical, protective and repulsive"; "I want to get out of this house, but at the same time I want to stay here forever"; "I felt he was both a friend and a stranger."

These oppositions pervade family relations throughout Ginzburg's fiction. Near the end of *Family*, Carmine experiences profound ambivalence toward his parents, who have come to visit Rome from their rural home in the Abbruzzo: "Carmine adored and detested their wrinkled faces, their long, straight, crepy necks, their black clothes and their knowing silence of old folks who have understood. They went home again, and it was an enormous weight off Carmine's shoulders to take them to the station and put them on the train. Yet at the same time, he felt the most heart-rending sadness." The translator Beryl Stockman renders accurately, if a bit clunkily, what Ginzburg needs a simple parallel construction to say—"*una enorme liberazione e una lacerante malinconia*" translated literally as "an enormous liberation and a lacerating melancholy"—but Carmine's disgust, love, relief, and sadness come through as "inextricably tangled" in English as they do in Italian.

If Ginzburg claims "the temporal dimension," with its attendant verb tenses, as the special province of writers, what about her evocations of simultaneity? She reflects on this latter tendency, not in her own writing but rather in the films of Fellini, such as *Casanova*: "everything is two-fold and ambiguous, in the regions of this story, or generally in Fellini's films: nothing is one thing, everything is double." She was particularly drawn to Fellini's *Satyricon*, which the director himself conceived of as a science-fiction film about ancient Rome, for its exploration of temporal obscurity: "In what era are we? It doesn't matter; we know at once that it doesn't matter, and that it's a new era for us, one unknown to our imagination." Ginzburg's immersion in Fellini's world of uncertainty, doubleness, and temporal disorientation can stand for her moviegoing—an experience that, as she repeatedly emphasizes, occurs in the dark. For all the joy she took in using such tenses as *l'imperfetto* and *il passato remote* to create a layered sense of human identity within time, Ginzburg also loved entering, by sitting in a darkened movie theater, a realm outside of time, a world of simultaneity and mystery: "True darkness brings us the true profundity of night and the true awareness of our human condition before the secrets of reality, secrets our thoughts find mysterious and full of a life that is intense, bewitched."

True darkness brings us the true profundity of night. Family ends with the words *la notte*, the night. I've said these novellas' deaths take place as unremarkably as other endings; however, I find the conclusion of *Family*, which occurs at some indeterminate moment before Carmine's death itself—but which is narrated in the past tense, that is, after Carmine has already died—to be the most intense, bewitching, and gorgeous passage in all of Ginzburg's work. Like the original, Stockman's translation relies on the imperfect and the past-perfect tenses to embody the drift of Carmine's memory and consciousness between moments in time:

Carmine now found himself gazing at his mother for long stretches, as she sat on the sofa in her black dress, and he remembered the times when they used to go to the neighbouring villages together, in search of bran for the pigs, because the war was on, and there was no bran to be found. He was a child then, and his mother was young. She had a full, pink face and white teeth. Her thick black hair was gathered into a fat bun studded with steel hairpins, and protruded from underneath her headscarf. He remembered one occasion when he was very tiny, still in his mother's arms, and they were in town, at the station. It was night time and pouring with rain. There were crowds of people with umbrellas waiting for the train, and mud was running between the tracks. Why on earth his memory should have squandered and destroyed so many days and so many events, and yet preserved that moment so accurately, bringing it safely through the years, tempests and ruins, he did not know. At that point, he could not remember anything about himself, what clothes and shoes he had worn, what wonder and curiosity had woven and unwoven itself in his thoughts at the time. His memory had thrown all that out as useless. Instead, he had retained a whole pile of random detailed impressions, that were hazy, but light as a feather. He had kept the memory of voices, mud, umbrellas, people, the night.

In a novella titled *Family*, I'm not surprised when a character clings to a memory of himself as a very young child "still in his mother's arms" as he approaches death, which, like the recalled night, looms obscurely before him. In memory, Carmine's mother protects him from the chaos of sense impressions around him on the train platform, a disorder that mirrors his present disorientation in the hospital room: "He never knew whether it was day or night, and he could never tell who was in the room and who had just left."

His mother's youthful vitality, in memory exemplified by her "white teeth," stands in contrast to the image of her, earlier in the novella, as an aging woman with "broken, black teeth." Indeed, the image of her black teeth, and the attendant discomfort Ivana, as well as Carmine's wife and mother-in-law, feel at that sight, recurs so often in the novella that it's hard, at this juncture, not to envision Carmine's youthful mother and aged mother as overlaid images that blur into each other, rather than as images in sequence—as, in *Satyricon*, "the old look like children, children [look] like the old."

The moments indicated by the paragraph's time-markers—"now," "then," "one occasion," "at the point"—merge into a single moment. Like the viewer of *Satyricon* in the darkened movie theater, Carmine apprehends "a whole pile of random detailed impressions," which, in turn, are transformed into a litany of barely connected words, a spell, a series

of signs and messages of the destiny that pursues human beings and urges them toward an unknown shore, along a way of life that nothing can stop; signs and messages it is impossible to see as either malign or beneficent, good and evil destinies being mingled and twisted together until they are inextricably alike.

le voci, il fango, gli ombrelli, la gente, la notte

"We'll still be here at midnight," said Angelica, "you wait and see."

—ERIC GUDAS
Los Angeles
January 2021

NOTE

I am deeply grateful to Stiliana Milkova for translating key passages from Natalia Ginzburg's 1975 essay "Il volto osceno della celluloide" expressly for this afterword, and for illuminating Ginzburg's use of verb tenses for me. The quotation from Italo Calvino appears in the 1961 essay "Natalia Ginzburg or the Possibilities of the Bourgeois Novel," which Professor Milkova and I cotranslated. Additional thanks go to Olivia Soule, who translated material from Einaudi's 2011 edition of *Famiglia*; although I did not use this material in my final version, I was glad to consult her translations.